THE GRADUATES

"You're very special to me, you know that, don't you?" asked Craig.

Jill turned toward him and brushed her lips against his cheek. "That's why I don't want to spoil things, Craig," she said. "I don't want to have to compete with all those other people and things. I'd rather be special to you, not someone you had to make time for between your music and your parties!"

"Jill, I don't think you should choose a college because you want to be near me," Craig said. "You have to choose a college because it's the best place for you."

"Ever since I saw Rosemont, I've dreamed of going there," Jill said. "I'd be crazy to turn it down." For the first time since the letter from Rosemont had arrived, Jill felt calm. She was sure that she was making the right decision.

Bantam Books by Janet Quin-Harkin
Ask your bookseller for the books you have missed

On Our Own

Sweet Dreams Romances

On Our Own
THE GRADUATES

Janet Quin-Harkin

BANTAM BOOKS
TORONTO · NEW YORK · LONDON · SYDNEY · AUCKLAND

RL 6, IL age 11 and up

THE GRADUATES
A Bantam Book / June 1986

Sweet Dreams and its associated logo are registered trademarks of Bantam Books, Inc. Registered in U.S. Patent and Trademark Office and elsewhere.

ISBN 0-553-25723-4

Published simultaneously in the United States and Canada

Bantam Books are published by Bantam Books, Inc. Its trademark, consisting of the words "Bantam Books" and the portrayal of a rooster, is Registered in U.S. Patent and Trademark Office and in other countries. Marca Registrada. Bantam Books, Inc., 666 Fifth Avenue, New York, New York 10103.

PRINTED IN THE UNITED STATES OF AMERICA

O   0 9 8 7 6 5 4 3 2 1

For my daughter Anne, that her own college days may bring her success, friends and fun.

ONE

"How many is that now?" Toni asked, looking up hopefully from behind the pile of envelopes.

Jill made a rapid count. "About a hundred and fifty."

Toni groaned. "I thought it was at least a thousand. We've been doing this forever. My tongue has so much glue on it that it sticks to my teeth every time I say a word that starts with *T-H*!"

Jill grinned. "I keep offering you a perfectly good sponge, but you insist on licking them," she said.

Toni looked across the table at Jill, suddenly serious again. "Tell me honestly," she said. "Do you think we'll finish by tonight?"

Jill sighed. "I don't know, Toni," she admitted. "It depends on how long we can keep going before we go crazy. I'm already beginning to see floating envelopes whenever I close my eyes. Why couldn't you have found yourself a nice, normal way to make money? You live only half a block from Burger King!"

1

Toni's blue eyes took on that lost, suffering look that everybody but Jill found hard to resist. "I thought I'd make so much more this way. We spent so much money in Europe this summer. I couldn't start college with no new clothes, could I? To stuff and lick a thousand envelopes a day sounded like a simple way to make a fortune!" She swept her arms out, and several dozen envelopes fluttered to the floor like oversized snowflakes.

Jill started laughing. Toni scowled at her, red faced.

"Sorry," Jill said. "I know I shouldn't laugh. But you have to admit, Toni, ever since second grade you've been a walking disaster area, and you probably always will be. I bet you'll do terrible things like knock someone's wheelchair down a hill when you're in the old folks' home."

Toni put on her proud, insulted expression. "For your information, Jill Gardner, I do not intend to spend my golden years in an old folks' home. You forget I'm going to be rich and famous. I'll be busy dividing my time between my penthouse in New York and my villa on the French Riviera."

"I hope your French has improved by then," Jill said sweetly. "Remember what almost happened to you several times when we were in France because of your marvelous command of the French language?"

"At least I didn't fall into a canal in Venice, the way some people did," Toni said. "That was crazier than *anything* I've ever done."

"You might have done the same thing if you'd seen someone . . ." Jill's voice trailed away, and she stared out of the window to where her father was working in the garden.

Toni leaned across the kitchen table and touched Jill's arm. "I'm sorry. That was dumb of me," she said. "I should learn to keep my mouth shut."

Jill managed to smile. "It's OK, Toni," she said. "I think I'm over Carlo now. The whole experience was so crazy and so unlike me. It all seems unreal, like a movie I was watching, instead of something that actually happened to me."

Toni nodded. "It was exciting, though, wasn't it? The whole month was exciting. It sure beat traveling with the French club, looking at museums and churches and staying in boring hotels."

Jill nodded in agreement. "I'm glad it's over, though. I've had enough excitement to last awhile. It's nice to know that our futures are planned out for the next four years. Now I can settle down to some peaceful studying."

"For once I happen to agree with you," Toni said. "Not about the peaceful studying part, of course, but I can't wait to get to college. Just think, thousands of new guys, all waiting to date me! Do you think I can date them all in four years?"

Jill laughed. "Toni, you're hopeless!" she said. "You have a one-track mind. Is that all you can think about—boys, boys, boys?"

"Not at all," Toni said, giving Jill a dramatic, withering stare. "Now that I am older and more mature, most of the time I think about men, men, men."

She laughed and Jill joined in. "Well, I have to think about something," Toni said. "I'm not the world's greatest student. I mean, I never actually enjoyed studying as you did. To tell you the truth, sometimes I get goose bumps just wondering if I can keep up with college work."

"Sure you can," Jill said warmly. "You can do anything that you're really interested in. And taking classes that really interest you is what college is about. Besides, I'll be there to help. At least with me as a roommate you'll have to do some studying. I'd hate to think what would happen to you if you were on your own."

Toni bent down to the big box at her feet and pulled out another pile of envelopes. "I'm glad we're going to room together," she said. "Just think of rooming with a complete stranger. You never know who you'd get. It might be someone who snored, or a complete workaholic who sat up all night studying, or a weirdo who walked in her sleep. Both of our lives might have been completely different if you'd gotten into that private college in Oregon," Toni said. "What was it—Hedgehill?"

Jill laughed. "Rosemont," she said, looking down at the letter she was folding. There was an uneasy silence as she continued to fold other letters.

Finally Toni asked, "Are you still disappointed about that, Jill? I thought you'd gotten over it."

Jill looked up and pushed her hair back from her face. "I have gotten over it," she said brightly. "It was the best thing that ever happened to me, getting turned down there. Now I can be with you and Craig, not struggling to keep up with a lot of grinds."

Then she went back to folding and stuffing again. Toni shook her head. "Selfishly speaking, I'm glad you didn't get in. I have a horrible feeling I might not make it through four years of college alone. But I do understand how much it must have hurt when they turned you down." She looked up with a grin. "Personally I've never been rejected by anyone, but I have a good imagination!"

"That's not true," Jill said, the frown disappearing from her forehead. "I remember when you got thrown out of the *Annie* chorus in seventh grade. You kept kicking Annie during the dance numbers."

"I knew I was meant for that role," Toni said. "Just think, if I'd had my lucky break as an actress then, I wouldn't have to face all these envelopes now!"

Jill nodded. "Sometimes I really envy Craig. He's so lucky to be a model. Imagine—ninety dollars an hour!"

"Craig's lucky," Toni agreed. "He's always happened to look like the world's youngest executive. A perfect model."

Jill smiled. "He looks perfect to me," she said.

Toni gave an exaggerated sigh. "How can you still manage to look goofy every time you talk about a guy you've known for over a year?"

Jill shrugged her shoulders and went back to her work. "I don't know," she said. "I guess it must be love!"

"Yuck!" Toni said. "No romantic attachments for me, thank you. I've got all of the State University at Thomson to date first! I'm taking your share of the guys, too, as long as Craig will be taking up your time."

"Help yourself," Jill said. "I have no desire to date thousands of other guys. They're all yours. It'll be wonderful to see Craig every single day." She looked up suddenly. "I wish they'd hurry and send our room assignment. I'm dying to know if we're in that block of dorms close to his frat house."

"I hope we get on that corner with the big oak tree," Toni said.

"So do I. It'll make the rooms nice and cool in hot weather."

"Who cares about weather? It'll also be easy to climb in and out at night," Toni said.

"But that's the great thing about college," Jill insisted. "You don't have to climb in and out. You'll be treated like an adult. You can come and go as you please." Jill looked at the pile in front of her and groaned. "Let's get done with these disgusting envelopes and then we can go up to my room and start planning how we'll decorate."

The girls were silently stuffing and sealing envelopes when the front doorbell rang a half hour later. Jill opened the door and was greeted by a smiling mailman holding a certified letter addressed to her. It was the first special delivery letter Jill had ever received. The long, slim envelope was decorated in the upper left-hand corner with a black crest—a rose tree growing on a mountain above the words "Rosemont College." Jill didn't realize her hands were trembling until she tried to rip the letter open.

"Dear Jill," it read.

We are pleased to inform you that your name has been removed from our waiting list and we are now able to offer you a place at Rosemont this fall. Please reply immediately by completing the attached forms if you wish to accept.

Information concerning tuition, fees, financial aid, and housing has been sent via first class mail and should arrive shortly.

We look forward to having you with us.

With best wishes,
Regina Perkins
Director of Admissions

Jill folded the letter and stuffed it into her jeans pocket.

"Who was that?" Toni asked, looking up from the envelope she was licking. "Anything exciting? A talent scout who wants to whisk me away from all this?"

"It was just the mailman," Jill said. "With some catalogs too big to go in the mailbox. Listen, Toni, I'm really getting a headache from all this envelope stuffing. Can we take a break for a while?"

"Sure," Toni began, glancing at her watch. "Oh, no! I had no idea we'd been doing this so long. No wonder my tongue feels like crepe paper. I'm supposed to be home now."

As Jill shut the door behind Toni, she felt a little guilty. She had never kept anything from her best friend. But she sensed that Toni wouldn't understand why the letter from Rosemont bothered her.

She was a little surprised herself to discover how much it had affected her. Her hands were still trembling as she made neat piles of the envelopes and letters Toni had left scattered around the floor. *What's wrong with you, anyway?* Jill asked herself as she paced nervously from the kitchen through the dining room to the living room. *You've made up your mind. It's too late to change.*

Jill wandered back toward the kitchen and into the bathroom. Her face was etched with nervousness. *I've got to get out of here*, she thought. *I don't want Mom and Dad to ask me a lot of questions.*

"Bye, Daddy," she yelled out the window to the backyard. "I'm going to take a walk."

"Have fun," her father called. "Be back for dinner."

Winding randomly beside the familiar neat houses without noticing them, Jill walked slowly along the neighborhood streets. A light rain began to fall, cutting the heat of the summer afternoon. It was the rain she had dreamed of on hot days in Italy. It fell as a fine mist, coating leaves and flowers and Jill's hair with beads of pearl. Jill's T-shirt was quickly damp, but she didn't mind. The rain and the gray sky harmonized with her mood.

Jill eventually reached the edge of the steep hill that led down to the waterside and the harbor far below her. Black islands dotted a gray, choppy ocean in front of her. To the west, the clouds merged with distant hills, the sky heavy with the promise of more rain to come. But the pressure inside her head wasn't coming from the approaching storm. An hour before she had known exactly where she was going. She had been looking forward to four years at college with close friends, close to home—a safe, comfortable future. Then one piece of paper had thrown everything into turmoil again.

She reached down and patted her pocket. She could feel the bulge of the letter against the tightness of her jeans. *Why did they have to do this to me now?* Jill thought angrily. Everything had been fine until the letter arrived. She had begun to look forward to attending the big state university. Then the letter reminded her of how much she had longed to sit in Rosemont's small classes among students as happy to be there as she was, to listen as the professor looked hard at her and said, "Good point, Ms. Gardner, I never thought of that."

Far across the harbor a lone tug crept between islands with a barge in tow. It gave a low, melancholy hoot as it passed out of sight. Jill sighed.

Her parents had taken her to visit Rosemont the fall of her senior year. She had been impressed by the ivy-covered walls of the main building, the spacious lawns and neatly kept flower beds, the musty smell of the library, the dark, rich paneling on the walls, and the old-fashioned classrooms. It had seemed to Jill everything a distinguished old college should be. The student who showed her around boasted about the small classes, the one-to-one discussions with professors, the festival of original plays, and the Halloween masked ball.

Her high school English teacher had arranged for her to meet the head of the English department. Dr. Barton had been a tall, distinguished woman who threw questions at Jill about her favorite Shakespearean play, the authors she loved and hated most, what she had written, and what she planned to write. She was so overpowering to Jill that Jill could only stammer answers that she knew sounded very childish and incoherent. Then Dr. Barton had told Jill that she had been highly recommended by her English teacher. "But," she continued, "I'm sure you know that our freshman class is very small, and we have to turn down many highly qualified applicants."

Jill had left not knowing whether or not to hope. For days afterward she had relived her interview, squirming with embarrassment at all her silly answers and thinking too late of witty and intelligent ones.

By April when nearly every college sent out its acceptances and rejections, Jill had persuaded herself that she would be happier at the state university closer to home, anyway. She began to look forward to being close to Craig and to being Toni's roommate. When the letter from Rosemont finally came, putting her on a waiting list, she had been disappointed, but not too surprised. The acceptance from State U. had arrived the same day, and Jill promptly filled out all the necessary forms and returned them.

"Well, I'm glad you're not going to that place," Craig had said when she told him the news. "They would have turned you into a real grind. I hear their biggest social event is nine o'clock break at the library. When I would have come down for the weekend, you'd have taken me on a tour of the reference room for some real excitement."

"Very funny," Jill had said, pushing him away and laughing in spite of her disappointment. "You know, I'm just so mad at Mr. Conway. If he hadn't persuaded me to apply to Rosemont, I'd never have wanted to go there."

Craig put his arms around her protectively. "Did you want to go there that much?" he asked.

Jill nodded, gazing up at him. "It was just such an *opportunity*. I've never seen a place like it before. You can almost feel the ideas and the creativity flying around, and it's so peaceful and secluded that I could have studied so much harder."

Craig smiled down at her. "And now it looks like you're stuck with boring old State U. and boring old me," he said.

She smiled back. "That was the one thing I was not looking forward to at Rosemont," she had whispered. "Being so far from you."

12

Then he had kissed her lightly on the nose, and they had walked home. Jill smiled, remembering that scene. At least Craig was happy she was going to State U. And Toni would never have applied to State U. without Jill. She had been thinking of taking classes at the community college until Jill had announced her own plans. There was no way she could let them both down.

State U. has a lot going for it, Jill thought. *It doesn't cost as much. It's closer to home. I'll be able to come home on some weekends. And Craig will be there. I'll be able to see him every single day. And I'll be rooming with Toni!*

TWO

"So, do you want to take this poster?" Toni asked the next day. She held up a picture of a dragon swooping over a hill.

"Too bright," Jill said.

"You said the one with the flowers was too bland," Toni said. "We have to make some decisions about what to take."

"Let's think about it first and then decide," Jill said. "It's hard to know until we see how much wall space we'll have."

"Boy, you're a grouch today," Toni said, flinging the poster onto Jill's bed. "I thought you wanted to get ready as much as I did. We have less than a month. What's bugging you?"

Jill had told neither Craig nor Toni about the letter from Rosemont. She had tried to push it from her mind. Shutting it out had not been easy. Jill was sure she had made the right decision to go to State U., but she knew that it was something she would wonder about for the rest of her life. She kept reading Robert Frost's poem about the road not taken.

I took the one less traveled by,
And that has made all the difference.

How much difference will it make? she wondered. Until then she had never really thought about how much she could control the course of her own life. She had gone through high school taking all the recommended classes, turning in her homework on time, and attending all the school-sponsored activities. She had applied to college because college was the next stage in life after high school. She had applied to Rosemont because a teacher suggested it and to State U. because it was close by. She had decided to attend State U. because Rosemont did not accept her. But she had never really chosen what to do with her life. The acceptance from Rosemont had forced her to make her first big decision, and it had been frightening.

"Doesn't it scare you, Toni?" she asked, rolling the poster up again and putting it back in its tube.

"What?" Toni asked, curling up comfortably like a cat on Jill's bed.

"Going to college!" Jill said. "It's just dawned on me that we've started on the first step down a long road and whatever choices we make now are going to affect us all our lives. Doesn't that worry you?"

Toni shrugged her shoulders. "Not particularly," she said. "You can always change your major if you change your mind. The only thing that scares me is passing exams. I'll have to think of a way for you to take them for me, or I'll get thrown out for sure."

She turned and looked at Jill critically. "Hey, don't worry so much," she said. "You've always been a worrier. I never worry, and I seem to survive just fine. So be like me. After all, college is not the end of the world. Plenty of people flunk college, or don't even go, and lead perfectly happy lives. Some even become rich and famous. And you'll be fine with your brain. It's not as if you're going to Rosemont where they only accept straight-A students. You'll sail through all your courses, and your professors will love you. You even have a boyfriend on campus waiting for you. You'll have a terrific time!"

Jill managed a smile. "I guess so," she said. "But I'm nervous, anyway." She gazed out the window. A lone motorbike was coming up the hill, accompanied by a loud pop-popping sound. "Isn't that your brother?" Jill asked.

Toni knelt on the bed. "Looks like him," she agreed. "I wonder what he wants. Not to tell me to come home for lunch, that's for sure. My mother's been worse than ever with this new sculpture of the creation she's working on. We wouldn't have eaten for days if I hadn't gone out and bought cans of ravioli."

"Well, he's definitely coming to get you," Jill said as the bike drew up to the curb.

Toni flung open the window before her brother could walk up the front path.

"Hi there, handsome!" she yelled loud enough to make Jill take a quick glance up and down the street to see if any of the neighbors were outside. Then she turned to Jill. "Well, what a disappointment. It's definitely not Romeo," she said so her brother could hear.

"Toni!" her brother called, looking up at the open window.

"Looking for me, Will?" she yelled back. "Or have you just come to see if Jill will feed you lunch?"

Will stood on the sidewalk, shading his eyes as he looked up at the window. "Toni, listen. You've got to come home now. Something's happened to Dad."

"What? What happened?" Toni shrieked.

"He collapsed at work, and they took him to the hospital. Mom's there now. She asked me to come and get you!"

"Oh, no," Toni moaned, sliding down from the bed. "Not Dad. I've got to go right now. Where did I put my shoes?"

"Here they are, Toni." Jill took her arm. "Are you going to be OK? Should I come with you?"

"You can't," Toni said, grabbing the shoes from her and trying to slip them on while still standing up. "You won't fit on the back of the motorbike. I've got to go, Jill. I'll see you later, OK?"

"Look, call if you need me," Jill said. "My mom should be back soon. I can borrow her car and come right over if you want. I hope everything's going to be OK."

"Toni, are you coming?" Will yelled from the street.

"I'm coming," Toni yelled back, rushing down the stairs two at a time and slamming the front door behind her.

Jill stood at the window watching Toni and Will go. She paced the room, putting away the debris that accompanied Toni wherever she went, mechanically plumping pillows, and straightening spreads until the room looked perfect again.

The telephone didn't ring all afternoon. By evening, Jill began to think of calling the Redmonds' house, but she was sure Toni would have called if she had wanted to talk. So she waited, growing increasingly nervous.

Toni didn't call until the next afternoon. Jill barely recognized the timid, soft voice on the other end of the line. "Jill?" Toni asked. "Can you meet me somewhere? I need to talk."

"How's your dad?" Jill asked. "Is he going to be all right?"

18

"He'll be OK eventually," came the small voice.
"But he had a heart attack," Toni said as though she
still didn't quite believe it. "Everything's a mess. I
don't know anything, Jill. I just need you over
here."

"I'll take Mom's car and come right over," Jill
said.

When Toni opened the front door, she looked
even smaller and more delicate than usual. Her
blond curls were unbrushed, and her eyes were
ringed by dark circles.

"I'm glad you're here," she said in a very
subdued voice. "Let's drive somewhere, OK?"

"Where do you want to go?"

Toni shrugged her shoulders. "Any old where.
Just around, so we can talk. I feel secure in cars."

They pulled away from the curb. "So tell me
everything," Jill said. "Did they let you see him
yet?"

"No, and they won't for a while," Toni said,
leaning forward with her head in her hands. "He's
still in intensive care. Even a mild heart attack is
pretty bad."

Toni leaned her head against the car window.
"You can't imagine how everything has changed
overnight," she said. "They told him he can't go
back to work again—at least not to his old job. He
can't do any more heavy lifting or hammering."

"Maybe they can find him a desk job, where he won't have to do any heavy work," Jill suggested. "He's worked for the same company for a long time. They won't just throw him out."

"But what else can he do, Jill?" Toni asked hopelessly. "You know my dad. He's good with his hands. I don't know how well he'd do in an office, even if they found him a job there. Anyway, he can't go back to work at all until the doctors say he can, and that might be months. My mom and Will and I sat up half the night talking, trying to make some plans for the future. I mean, my mother can't support the whole family on her sculptures, can she? She says we'll get some insurance or compensation or something from the union, and we'll have to make do with that for a while. She can't go out and get a job yet because someone will have to take care of Dad. It's hopeless."

"It only seems that way right now, Toni," Jill said softly. "It'll all work out, I bet. Most people lead really normal lives after a heart attack now."

"But it won't work out for me, that's what I'm trying to say, Jill," Toni said. "My mother and I discussed it last night. I can't go to college with you."

"Not go to college?" Jill stammered. "Why not?"

Toni shrugged her shoulders. "How can I? I can't take money from my parents right now, and I don't have any of my own."

"Oh," Jill said, trying to digest this while her stomach felt as if it were falling down a well. "Oh, Toni, I didn't think of that. But you have to go to college. There must be a way. There are work-study programs and loans and things like that. You can tell the scholarship people what happened."

"It won't work right now, Jill," Toni said evenly. "It's more than just money, anyway. I couldn't concentrate on anything. I'd be thinking about my family when I was supposed to be memorizing poetry. Besides, they need me at home. Someone has to help Mom take care of Dad. It's only fair that Will gets to finish college, so that leaves me."

Jill pulled the car over to the side of the road, parking under the shadow of a huge oak. "But what will you do, Toni?" she asked.

"I'll try to go to the community college here," she said, "and get a part-time job. That way I can transfer to State U. when things look better."

Jill reached across and touched Toni's hand. Toni continued to stare ahead. "I'm really sorry, Toni," Jill whispered. "I wish there was something I could do or say to make you feel better."

"It's OK," Toni said. "Things will have to get better, I suppose."

"They will, Toni. I know they will. You're the strongest person I know. And you can always count on me when you want someone to talk to."

Toni turned to look at her friend for the first time. "You'll be away," she said. "We'll be apart for the first time. You'll have to find a new roommate. Maybe now you can get yourself someone who's as neat as you. Maybe it's for the best really. Maybe I would have driven you crazy after a couple of months and our friendship would have broken up."

"Oh, Toni," Jill said, brushing away her tears. "You could never drive me crazy. You're the one who keeps me sane. I don't even know if I want to go to college if you're not going to be there."

"Don't be dumb," Toni said, sounding more like her usual forceful self for the first time that day. "Things will be much better for you without me. You'd have been wasting all your time trying to help me with my bonehead English. Now there's nothing to stop you from graduating magna cum laude, whatever that is. And you'll be a professor and win a Nobel prize, and you'll say, 'I owe it all to my old friend Toni, who didn't come to college with me when we were both eighteen.'"

"You're crazy," Jill said, smiling now and reaching over to hug her friend. "But I know one thing, Toni. However long it takes, you'll be in the middle of some wild adventure again soon, and this whole thing will be a memory."

"I hope you're right, Jill," Toni said, sinking back in her seat again. Then, seeing the tears in Jill's eyes, she laughed. "I'll have to be back to normal soon. Otherwise, who'll take care of you?"

THREE

Jill played with a french fry on the plate in front of her, absently drawing pictures with it in the small pool of ketchup.

"You seem a million miles away right now," Craig said. Jill looked up, startled. For a moment she almost had forgotten where she was. Craig was leaning against a bench at the Burger Palace, looking tanned and relaxed. He looked even more handsome than when Jill had first met him. Most of the summer in the Alaskan air, paddling canoes and chopping trees as a bit player in a wilderness movie, had given him a rugged, muscular appearance.

Jill couldn't contain a smile, even as she sighed. Craig's presence alone managed to make her worries seem less troublesome. "I just can't stop thinking about Toni. Now that things are really rough for her, there's nothing I can do to help."

Craig reached across and took Jill's hand, giving it a warm, reassuring squeeze. "Don't worry," he said. "It'll all get better faster than you think. After all, she has a place at State U. She can always transfer when things improve at home. And if she does this year at the community college, she won't get left behind."

"I know," Jill said. "I guess I just feel guilty that everything is going smoothly for me and not for her. It's just not fair!"

Craig smiled at her. "One of your biggest faults, well, maybe your only fault, is that you spend too much time worrying. You've always worried about Toni, even when she isn't worrying about herself. Just stop worrying about things you can't change. You won't make it any easier for Toni if she sees how upset you are."

Jill looked up at him and smiled. "You're right," she said.

"Oh, I know," Craig said, flashing her a teasing grin. "I'm a warm and wonderful human being, not to mention cute!"

"To say nothing of modest," Jill quipped, her depression slipping away.

Craig grinned. "At least I got you laughing," he protested. "You looked as if you'd never smile again when I walked in here."

"I know," Jill said, picking up a french fry and eating it even though it was cold. "I guess I was scared about my own future, too. I'm just realizing that it's a really big step to go away from home for the first time, to choose the right college."

"Well, you've done all right so far," Craig said. "You'll have a great time at State U. There are great people and hundreds of parties and so many courses that you won't even know what to take."

"I'll be bugging you for advice all the time," Jill said.

"You'd better not bug me too much," Craig said, teasing her. "I'm taking a pretty heavy load this year. I'll give you official bugging hours. After all, if you'd gone to another college, you wouldn't have me around, and you'd do just fine."

"Well, I don't intend to hang around you every minute," Jill said. "It's just that I'll be on my own, without even Toni, for the first time, and sometimes I'm going to need to yell, 'Help, what do I do now?' And I want someone to be there to answer."

"If you think everyone in college is cool and mature, you're in for a shock," Craig said. "Didn't I ever tell you about the baby race, when the guys all crawled across the lawn in diapers with pacifiers in their mouths? There are a lot of crazy people in college, and they act even crazier because they're away from home for the first time. You should see some of the things that go on in my frat house—or maybe you shouldn't." He laughed. "That reminds me—I meant to ask you before—do you want to come to a party one of my frat brothers is giving tomorrow? Dick called last night. His family has a cottage on some little island, and he's giving a huge party there. It should be wild."

"Too wild for a sheltered girl like me?" Jill asked sweetly.

"It'll give you a good idea of what life will be like at State U.," he said. "If you can take this party, you'll survive OK."

"You make it sound like a test," Jill said. "But I'd like to come, anyway. I've hardly met any of your college friends yet.

"I hope they like me." Jill said as she huddled close to Craig. The ferry to the island was open, and the wind was blowing hard. In spite of the big wool sweater she wore, Jill was chilled by the wind and the cold mist that sprayed up over the side of the boat.

Craig squeezed her close to him. "You make it sound as if I'm taking my future bride home to meet the family," he said. "It's only the Sigmas. What does it matter whether they like you or not? I like you, and that's the main thing. In fact, I don't want them to like you too much. I don't want to have to fight for you at school!"

Jill snuggled close to Craig, feeling the warmth of his shoulder against her tingling cheek. *I am lucky,* she thought.

She was a little scared of meeting all Craig's friends, however. Until then Craig had existed for

Jill in a little capsule, consisting of his family, Jill's home, and Seattle. She felt secure with this Craig. For the first time Jill was going to see Craig outside of their little capsule, surrounded by his friends, part of a world she didn't yet know.

The sun was just setting beyond Vancouver Island as the boat glided into shore. The front of the ferry was lowered with a hollow clang onto the concrete and people began to stream off. Craig took Jill's hand, and they followed a small, winding path across the dunes.

Ahead of them a huge fire was already crackling on the beach, sparks leaping up into the pink sky, and the smell of wood smoke drifting toward them. Figures were moving around the fire, and a great roar of laughter went up just before someone noticed them.

"Well, look who's here!" he yelled to the others. "None other than the man himself."

"Plus a pretty girl," someone else added.

"Naturally," came a third voice.

"So you actually got back from Alaska," the first boy said, stepping forward to meet them. "We were all set to send out an expedition to look for your whitened bones."

"Oh, come on, Murphy," someone else said. "You know Craig. When he does something, he does it in style. I bet he spent the whole time at the

Alaska Hilton and worked his way through all the lovely young starlets!"

"Cut it out, guys," Craig said, coughing the way he did when he was embarrassed. "It was murder up there. There were no starlets! There were only two females, and they were both over forty-five. One was the producer's wife and the other the wardrobe lady. We spent all our spare time slapping mosquitoes. Jill can tell you. I wrote about the horrors to her."

Jill could feel several pairs of eyes focus on her. "So you're the famous Jill?" a sandy-haired boy asked. "We finally get to meet you. We thought you were someone he had invented to keep us quiet."

"No, we didn't." The second boy, slightly round, with a mass of dark curly hair, interrupted. "We saw her picture up on his bookcase."

"That could have been anyone's picture," the first boy said, laughing. "Craig would go up to any strange girl and ask if he could take her picture."

"Probably tells them all he's a movie star!" the third boy joined in, and they all laughed.

Craig turned to Jill. "Don't listen to a thing these guys tell you," he said, laughing. "This is Dick who owns the cottage, and these two are Jeff and Murphy. I think his first name is something like Jeremy, but only his mother remembers for sure."

"Why don't you guys come into the cottage where the food and drink is," Dick said, walking ahead of them. "We have the ribs all ready to barbecue when Toad's gang gets here."

At that moment there were shouts from across the dunes, and figures appeared in the distance, waving frantically.

"Speak of the devil," Dick said. "Here they are now!"

A girl whose long hair hung below her waist ran across the lawn to Dick and wound her arms around his neck.

"Darling, it is so good to see you!" she said. "So this is your summer home. I've been wanting to come round ever since you first told us about it." She broke away from him. "Tell me, does anyone notice my English accent? I spent two glorious months in England getting a huge dose of culture. I didn't realize how many churches and museums existed before. Now I know all about English history, and Craig won't have to write my papers for me anymore!" She looked around her. "Is he here yet?" She turned so swiftly that her hair flew out like a veil behind her. "Oh, there you are darling." She screamed and rushed over to Craig, flinging her arms around him. Jill was standing right beside him, still holding his hand. "I've missed you every moment," she whispered.

"Don't mind Janine," Dick whispered to Jill. "She's like that with everyone. She's a theater major."

Jill felt her stomach twisting into a tight knot. Craig had never mentioned anyone called Janine before.

"Come on, Janine," Dick said loudly. "You're keeping Craig from the drink I was about to get him. And I want him to help me put on the ribs."

"Since he's the only person in the entire house who can cook anything other than baked beans," one of the other boys added. "Yeah, come on, Janine, release the cook!"

Craig freed himself from her arms and followed Dick into the house. Jill stood there alone.

"Hi, there. I don't think we've met before." Jill turned to see one of the boys who had arrived with Janine. "You never came to the house, did you?"

"She looks familiar to me," a second boy added. "Weren't you at that party when they set fire to the bed?"

Jill shook her head. "I came with Craig," she said.

"Did I meet you on that marine biology weekend?" the first boy asked. "When the boat capsized and we had all those starfish? Is Craig going to take marine biology again this year?"

"I don't know," Jill said. "This will be my first semester at State U." *I have no idea what subjects he is taking,* she thought. There was suddenly so much she didn't know about him. Perhaps there was a large part of his life that he didn't want her to share. Perhaps she belonged only in a compartment marked "Jill," to be taken out on occasional Saturday nights and vacations and then put back again.

"Excuse me?" she asked, aware suddenly that she had been staring into the darkness and that the boys were still trying to make conversation.

"I asked if you'll be coming to the football games this year. I know Craig was thinking of joining the band with us. Do you play an instrument?"

"No, I don't," Jill said.

"Too bad," the first boy said. He looked around. "Hey, isn't that Angie with Rom in there? I've got to tell her what happened after she went home that night!"

"Yeah, let's go in. It's getting cold out here," the other boy added. "You want to find some food?" he asked Jill politely.

Jill followed, although she was certain that the boys were looking for an excuse to get away from her. A moment of panic swept through her at the thought of standing alone all evening. Then she turned and saw Craig glancing in her direction.

"Oh, there you are," Craig called, coming out to meet her. "I thought you were with me when we went in. What happened—did we get swept apart in the tide?"

"Something like that," she said, taking the hand he held out to her.

"Look, Jill, don't take these guys too seriously," he said in a low voice. "They like to brag and exaggerate. You know how it is. Just don't take anything they say seriously."

"You mean the part about your being smooth?" she asked, smiling up at him.

"About anything you hear tonight," Craig said. "Come on, your hands are freezing. You need some hot nachos."

The small, rough pine room was packed wall to wall with people. The noise level made normal conversation impossible. Jill shrank back against Craig.

"Does everyone always shout in your frat house?" she asked.

"What?" he yelled, laughing at her.

"I asked if they were always this noisy."

"This?" Dick asked, joining in. "This is quiet. You should hear them after a football game! The food's on the table, drinks are in the kitchen. Now I've done my duty as a host. Help yourselves or starve."

Then he wormed his way through the crowd, leaving Jill feeling like a sardine packed in beside Craig and a dozen people she didn't even know.

"You were very quiet tonight," Craig said on the ferry going home.

"It's just that everyone else was so noisy," Jill said. "I hardly had a chance to talk."

"But they are good guys, aren't they?" Craig asked. "You'll get to know them better when you come to our parties at school."

Jill took a deep breath. "I don't know if I'll be coming to many parties," she heard herself say.

"Why not? You didn't have a good time?"

"It's not that, Craig," she said evenly. "It's just that I've been having second thoughts about where I go to college."

"What do you mean?" Craig asked, startled. "You're coming to State U., aren't you?"

"I thought I was," Jill said. "But tonight I've been doing some serious thinking. You remember Rosemont College in Oregon, don't you? You know how much I wanted to go there until they put me on their waiting list. Well, they've let me know that a place has opened up for me."

"Congratulations," Craig said. "That's terrific, Jill."

Jill shifted her feet uneasily. She had expected Craig to protest, to beg her to reconsider. She looked out past him to the white trail of water behind the ferry boat. "I didn't think I wanted to go there anymore because you and Toni were more important to me than any college. But now Toni can't go, and tonight it suddenly hit me that it might be better for both of us if I weren't at college with you."

"What are you trying to say?" Craig asked uneasily. "You don't like my friends?"

"No, Craig. I thought your friends were fun. It's just that I realized tonight that you have a whole life apart from me. You have interests that aren't my interests and friends that aren't my friends. Maybe it would be best for both of us if we didn't . . . " Jill's voice trailed off.

Craig reached his arm around Jill's shoulders. "You're very special to me, you know that, don't you?" he said.

Jill turned toward him and brushed her lips against his cheek. "That's why I don't want to spoil things, Craig," she said. "I don't want to have to compete, every day, with all those other people and things. I'd rather be special to you, not someone you had to make time for between your music and your parties and your Janines!"

He laughed. "Well, she's one person you really don't have to worry about. Biggest flirt on the campus, and everybody knows it."

"But I don't want to spend my life feeling jealous when I see you with other girls," Jill said.

"Jill, I don't think you should choose a college because you do or you don't want to be near me or any guy," Craig said. "You have to choose a college because it's the best place for you to get the education you want."

"Ever since the day I saw Rosemont, I've dreamed of going there," Jill said. "I'd be crazy to turn it down." For the first time since the letter from Rosemont had arrived, Jill felt calm. She was sure that she was making the right decision to go to Rosemont.

FOUR

"Here, don't forget these," Toni said.

Jill reached out, then stopped in surprise. "Toni, what would I need with flippers?"

"You never know," Toni said. "One of the boys may have a private plane, and he may fly you all over to Hawaii for the weekend, and you don't want to be the only one without flippers, do you?"

"If that happens, I'll treat myself to a new pair in Hawaii," Jill said, stuffing the flippers back into her closet. "Honestly, Toni, if I took everything you wanted me to, there wouldn't be any room for me."

"I just want you to be prepared for anything," Toni said. "You don't want to be left out because you're the only without a surfboard or ice skates!"

"Toni, I don't even own a surfboard or ice skates, and I'm going to have to do some hard studying to keep up with all those people. I won't have time for flying around the country surfing or ice skating!"

"I just want you to belong, Jill," Toni said, picking up one of Jill's stuffed animals from her bed. "I don't want you to feel like an outsider."

Jill looked up from the suitcase she was packing and smiled. "Don't worry about me, Toni. You've got enough worries of your own right now." She picked up her old teddy bear from the bed. "Do you think it's OK to take one of my stuffed animals?"

"Why not?" Toni demanded.

Jill flushed. "They might laugh at me."

"Of course they won't. I bet everyone brings stuffed animals. Hey, that's an idea." Toni started laughing. "You could always take me. I wouldn't mind sitting at the foot of your bed all day, doing nothing. It sure beats cleaning bathrooms and doing laundry." She propped herself up on the bed, arms stuck out like a stuffed animal, a wistful smile on her face.

"OK. You're hired," Jill said. "Go pack yourself in my suitcase." She laughed as she looked down at Toni. "Oh, Toni, I wish you were coming with me."

Jill walked to her closet and stood frowning at it. "Why do none of my clothes seem right for an exclusive college?" she muttered.

"Maybe because they came exclusively from discount stores!" Toni quipped.

"They did not," Jill said quickly. "But they all look like fifth grader's clothes. I bet everyone else will look as if they stepped out of *Vogue*."

"No, they won't," Toni said. "Trendy people wear stuff from thrift shops or army surplus."

"But I don't have anything like that, either," Jill said. "Ordinary, that's what describes my wardrobe. Good old ordinary Jill." She pulled down her favorite pleated gray pants, several pairs of jeans, and her one dressy dress. "This is it, I suppose."

"So you're not taking your French blouse?" Toni asked.

"Oh, I'll take that," Jill said. "I haven't had a chance to wear it yet. It's so formal. But I hope there'll be some time when I want to look really elegant." She picked up the delicate lace blouse from its hanger and laid it across the top of her other clothes.

"Don't forget your slippers," Toni said. "Colleges always have cold floors." She handed Jill her fluffy boots, and Jill slipped them down the side of the case.

"And your ski boots," Toni added, rummaging in the back of the closet.

"Toni! Will you stop it!" Jill said, laughing. "I'll be back for Thanksgiving, way before the start of the ski season. Besides, I can hardly ski. I don't want to do anything that makes me look like a fool." She took out a neatly folded pile of underwear and put it into the case.

"Gee, it's embarrassing to see how neat your drawers are." Toni peered over Jill's shoulder into the drawer. "What if your roommate is a slob?"

"I hope not," Jill said.

"Do you know who she's going to be yet?"

"Since I was admitted late, I don't find out until I get there."

"So you'll only discover then it's too late if she's a slob or a weirdo."

Jill shut the case firmly. "Stop it, Toni. You're starting to make me nervous again. Anyway, I've survived living in a room with you, and there can't be much bigger slobs or weirdos around!"

"Thanks a lot," Toni said. "That's what I get for coming over to help! I might as well go home."

"No, Toni, don't do that," Jill said. "This might be the last chance we have to be together for a while."

"You mean you've changed your mind about inviting me to dinner tonight?" Toni asked, staggering across the room with a pile of books in her arms.

"Of course not. But you know what it will be like tonight. My sister's kids will be knocking over their milk and fighting over the biggest piece of cake. We won't get much time to talk."

"What about Craig?" Toni asked. "Will he be here?"

"He's stopping by later," Jill said.

Toni grinned. "When Stephanie's monsters have gone home. Smart guy!"

Jill mechanically took the books from Toni and put them, one by one, into a big carton.

"I can't help it," Jill said, still packing books. "I like my books. They'll make me feel as if I'm not so far from home."

"Toni looked around the room. "Everything looks so bare," she said. "Look how bright the wallpaper is where your ballerina print used to be."

Jill followed Toni's gaze. "That poster hung there for five years. Now I really know I'm going," she said. "This is the last time this will ever be my room."

"You make it sound as if you're going into the army or something," Toni said. "You'll be back for vacations."

"I know," Jill said. "But it will never be the same again. It will never be my own special, secure place because half my stuff will be somewhere else. I'm going to be out on my own, Toni! And Mom and Dad won't be around for me to run to when I need them, and I'll have to make my own decisions."

"Lucky you," Toni said. "Just think—you won't ever have to tell people where you're going or what time you'll be home. You'll be treated like an adult."

"Yeah," Jill said.

"You don't sound very excited," Toni said. "If I were you, I'd be jumping all over the place."

"Adults do not jump," Jill said sedately. "And part of me is excited, but part of me is also very scared. It's a big step, Toni."

"You're going to do just fine, Jill," Toni insisted. "You're going to get wonderful grades, and everyone's going to be proud of you, and you'll probably write a novel, and they'll make you a professor, and I'll be able to say, 'I used to know her way back when. In fact, I helped her pack up her things before she went away to be famous.'"

"Oh, shut up," Jill said, hurling a book past Toni and laughing. "Here, help me shut this. This is the last one. Then we'd better go down and help my mom set the table."

Toni bounced obediently on the suitcase until Jill snapped it shut. "That's it," she said, leaping up again. "All packed and ready to go in the morning. I'm starving. Let's go and hurry dinner along." She ran down the stairs ahead of Jill.

Jill paused to look around her room. Stripped of almost everything that was hers, it looked strange and unfamiliar. "Out on my own," she whispered to herself as she turned to follow Toni.

Jill's sister and her family arrived soon afterward, and the family sat down to one of her mother's special dinners.

"It's not Thanksgiving," seven-year-old Andrea exclaimed scornfully as Jill's father carried in the turkey.

"I know, but Aunt Jill loves turkey," Jill's mother explained. "We wanted all her favorite things for dinner."

"I want a drumstrick. Can I have a drumstick, Grandpa?" five-year-old Mark demanded.

"Sit in your seat and behave yourself," Stephanie's husband, Jim said firmly. "And you, too, Andrea."

Toni caught Jill's eye across the table. Jill attempted to smile. She was secretly wishing that she and Toni could have slipped away to have pizza somewhere. She looked down at her huge plate of food and suddenly realized that she wasn't hungry. *I love them all,* she thought. *But I wish they'd all go away tonight. Even my parents are getting on my nerves.*

"Aren't you glad you'll be at Rosemont tomorrow?" Toni asked as they carried out the plates together. "Whenever you start to feel homesick, just think of dear little Andrea shooting her baked potato into your lap."

Jill smiled as she looked back toward the dining room. "I didn't mean to yell at her," she said. "It's just that I'm feeling so nervous, and they're being so noisy tonight. Family dinners are always a pain."

"Don't worry," Toni said. "You only have to survive the cake and ice cream, and then Craig will magically appear to sweep you away from all this."

"If I know Craig," Jill said, smiling, "he'll magically appear in time for the cake and ice cream. He can't resist my mother's desserts."

The doorbell rang, as if on cue, and both girls were laughing as they carried out the ice cream. Half an hour later Craig and Jill left to drive Toni home.

"You should thank me for giving you the perfect excuse to escape," Toni said, laughing. "Thanks for the ride. I'll be around in the morning to say goodbye, Jill." She waved and ran toward her house.

"It's going to be hard for you not having her around," Craig commented as they drove off.

"I know it," Jill agreed. "I'm going to miss everyone so much."

"Not your niece and nephew, I hope," Craig said, laughing. "My kids are not going to grow up to be brats. I want everyone to say what well-behaved children they are and what a pleasure it is to have them around. Just like their father!"

Jill laughed uneasily. It always unsettled her when Craig talked about the future, even if it was a joke. Craig turned to look at her. "There is so much future ahead," he said quietly. "Does it scare you, too—just thinking about it?"

"Sometimes," Jill agreed. "Especially tomorrow—right now."

"Oh, you'll be fine," Craig said, reaching across to take her hand. "You'll have a great time at Rosemont. I know it. Just don't have too great a time without me there. I don't want to spend my entire life feeling jealous."

"You won't have to, Craig," Jill said softly, stroking his hand.

"I was just thinking," he said quietly, "that I should have persuaded you to stay at State U. with me. I might have made the biggest mistake of my life."

"Let's not talk about that again," Jill said in a shaky voice. "I've managed to convince myself that I've made the right choice. You won't have any reason to be jealous, Craig. You don't have to worry about me."

They drove on in silence. Then Craig said, "Jill, I don't want you to feel trapped. You know what I mean? I want you to feel free at college—"

"To date other people, you mean?" she asked haltingly.

"If that's what you want," he said. "I don't want you to miss out on good times because of me, and if you meet someone else and you'd like to go out with him, well, we both still have a lot of maturing to do. We might change and become different people by the time we're through college."

"I guess we might," Jill said. *As if I could ever stop loving you, Craig*, she thought.

"Of course we might decide that we belong together," Craig went on. "But by then we'll have had enough experience to make the right choice."

"Sure," Jill said. *You might*, she thought. *I will have spent four years of college thinking about you.*

"I'm glad we're being so mature about this," Craig said as he pulled the car to a halt on a quiet

44

side road. "It's very important for people to know where they stand in a relationship."

He turned off the engine, then took her in his arms and kissed her again and again. When they finally drew apart, he whispered, "I've just decided that if you ever look at another guy, I'm going to break every bone in his body!"

"Oh, Craig," Jill said, laughing. "I love you so much. I'm going to miss you every second we're apart."

FIVE

Jill had just gone out to start loading the car when she saw a large box with legs come staggering along the sidewalk.

"Toni?" Jill asked hesitantly.

"Who did you think it was at this hour?" came Toni's muffled voice.

"But what are you carrying?" Jill asked, staring in dismay as Toni put down her box.

"I've been asking my brother for last-minute suggestions on things you can't do without," she said. "So I brought some of them."

"Toni, I'll never get them in the car. What are they?" Jill asked, not knowing whether to laugh or to cry over her friend's thoughtfulness.

Toni stood there on the sidewalk like a magician. "Item number one," she said, producing it from the box like a rabbit from a hat. "One popcorn popper. Very good for heating soup, hot chocolate, or instant oatmeal. Or for making popcorn if you want to be very boring.

"Item two, bag of food supplies to keep off starvation."

"Toni, I've already paid for full board at the college, and they don't allow us to cook in our rooms or even pop popcorn."

"You just wait," Toni said darkly. "According to my brother, students die of starvation all the time. They take one look at the meals in the college cafeteria and never eat again."

"Rosemont won't be like that," Jill said confidently.

"Ha!" Toni said. "You just take my bag of food to be on the safe side. You might make a fortune selling it to other starving students."

Jill laughed as she stuffed the bag into the trunk of the car. "You make it sound as if Rosemont is in the middle of the wilderness," she said. "If I'm hungry, I can walk to the nearest supermarket, you know. But thanks for thinking of me."

"There's more," Toni said, handing Jill a plastic shopping bag. Jill opened it cautiously, then almost dropped it.

"Pets aren't allowed, Toni. What is it?"

Toni looked offended. "It's not a pet, it's my grandmother's fur cape." She reached into the bag and drew out a long, dark piece of fur. "I want you to take it so you can look right on formal evenings." She handed it to Jill.

"I can't take this, Toni," Jill said, stroking it hesitantly. "I'd be scared something would happen to it."

"No, take it," Toni said. "When would I ever get a chance to wear it? And if the president ever comes to Rosemont, you're going to need something for the banquet. I want him to look around the room and notice you." Her voice was flat, but she was grinning as she spoke.

Jill shook her head and handed back the fur. "Toni, I don't know what I'm going to do without you," she said. "I also don't know where I'm going to put everything in my room. They're large as dorm rooms go, but not that large. And only one small chest each. I hope my roommate doesn't bring much stuff, or we'll have to sleep out in the hall."

"You might meet interesting people that way," Toni said. "Guys can't help but notice you if they have to step over you."

"I don't want guys to notice me," Jill said. "I've already got Craig, remember?"

"College is a time to spread your wings and experiment—isn't that what they were always telling us in school?" Toni asked. "You should experiment, before you wind up a boring old housewife."

"Toni, I do not intend to be a boring old housewife for four years at least," Jill said, laying her tennis racquet on top of the various boxes and bags, then slamming the trunk shut.

"So you're really going to Rosemont!" Toni said as Jill pulled the keys from the lock. "For the first time in ten years, I won't be able to just run around the block and up the hill to come cruising into your kitchen begging your mom for chocolate-chip cookies."

Jill's mouth curved downward. "I know. But that part hasn't really hit me yet. Do you realize we've never been apart for more than a two-week summer vacation?" Then her face brightened again. "One thing's for sure. My mother will be furious if you don't stop by at least once a week for chocolate-chip cookies."

Toni laughed. "Maybe I could convince her to send you one or two a month. They're excellent brain food, I read." Then her expression grew serious. "Let's hope you don't change, Jill," she said. "Strange things have been known to happen to people when they go to places like Rosemont. I don't want us to drift apart. I don't want you to come home for vacations and not have time for nobodies who go to community colleges."

"As if I'd do that," Jill said. "I'd do anything to make things easier for you right now, Toni. I'd even turn down Rosemont and stay here with you if I thought it would do any good."

"Thanks, Jill," Toni said. "But right now there is nothing you can do."

"Have you signed up for classes yet?" Jill asked.

"Not yet," Toni said. "Their quarter doesn't start until the end of September, so there's no rush. I don't really want to make any decisions right now. I know I need a job, and I know I'd better enroll at college, but I can't do anything until they tell me Dad is going to be all right. So right now my life is on hold."

Jill was flooded by a rush of affection for her best friend. She wanted to reach out and give her a hug. But she knew Toni would only laugh at her silly sentimentality, so she fought back her tears.

"Jill, where are you?" her mother's voice called from the front door. "Oh, you're out there already. And there's Toni. How nice. I'd better tell your father we're ready to load up the car!"

"It's already done, Mom," Jill called back.

Half an hour later Jill, her mother, and her father set off, all three in the front seat, the backseat full of Jill's lamp and her stereo. Toni waved madly from the sidewalk. Jill could see her still waving as they turned the corner.

"Bye, Toni," she whispered. Although she felt a lump forming in her throat, Jill managed to fight off the tears that burned her eyes—until her mother looked over and handed her a tissue. Once the first tears flowed, Jill was helpless to stop them. She leaned against her mother's shoulder and sobbed quietly, until her mother finally teased her.

"Jill, you'll have to stop crying soon, or your father will be in such a state that we'll have to pull off the road!" Jill laughed when she saw through her own pink eyes that her father's eyes glistened with tears.

By the time they stopped for lunch, she had stopped crying and her nose had faded back to its usual color. She could manage to swallow only a large diet soda.

They arrived at Rosemont in the early afternoon. The campus appeared even more impressive than Jill had remembered it. Huge stone pillars, each with a stone lion sitting on top, straddled a forbidding looking gateway. On either side of the pillars were high hedges. In front of one of the hedges was a sign, tastefully carved in stone: "Rosemont College, Established 1887." From the gate, the road curved up a slope covered in rhododendron bushes, until it came out to the flat area where the main college buildings stood. The administration building stood behind green, manicured lawns. It was four floors high and ivy covered.

"Is this where we have to go?" her mother asked in a voice that sounded as frightened as Jill felt.

Jill consulted her welcome package again. "It says Hollister Hall," she said doubtfully. "'All freshmen should report to Hollister Hall for room assignments,' it says. Hollister is one of the dorms. It's behind the main buildings and to the right, if I'm reading this map properly."

"Let me see," her father said, taking it from her. "Yes, that's it. Hollister. So we follow the road around here. Oh, yes, there's a sign pointing right to it." He seemed so relaxed that Jill instantly regretted all the times she had refused his help or regarded it as an interference. *Dad's always been around to take care of me,* she thought. *Now he's going away. I don't think I want to go to college after all!*

The car crunched across gravel and came to a halt outside a second, ivy-covered building. This one was more like Dracula's castle. Jill recognized it as Hollister by the round turret in one corner. As she got out of the car she caught sight of the view—the Columbia River glinting in one direction and Mount Hood far off in the other. It was a beautiful spot. It suddenly struck Jill that she was going to gaze at that view every day for the next four years. Four years of absorbing the greatest words ever written, the deepest thinking ever thought in majestic, peaceful surroundings!

No sooner had Jill thought it than a girl burst screaming from Hollister, leaped down the front steps, and was about to run off across the gravel when a boy hurtled down after her, yelling, "I'm going to get you for this, you wait and see." They both took off in a spray of gravel, leaving Jill and her parents staring after them in amazement.

Another girl appeared from the front door, looked at the running couple, then down at Jill's family. "Don't mind them," she said calmly. "She plays the same joke on him at the start of every semester. And every time he falls for it. You must be a new freshman. I'm Sandy Shaw on the welcoming committee. Why don't you come inside?"

Inside, the building was very dark and cool. Their feet echoed down the length of a stone-tiled hall until they were shown into a large circular room, obviously the room below the turret. "This is the round room," Sandy said. "It's set up to be our freshman reception room today. You'll be coming back here for the meeting at five."

The room was furnished with several non-matching sofas, heavy red velvet drapes, and a TV set in a corner. It also contained a nineteenth-century statue of a man on a marble stand and several old photographs of Rosemont. It reminded Jill of a badly furnished antiques store. It also had, for the day, a long table set up near the door with several students seated at it. Signs in front of them divided the alphabet among them. Jill automatically went to the serious-looking boy with heavy-rimmed glasses behind the sign marked "E-H" and introduced herself.

"Gardner," the boy said, flicking through papers. "Gardner, now where is it?"

For a terrible moment Jill wondered if there had been a mistake. All the information that had been sent to her was intended for a different person. A computer had printed her name in the wrong spaces, and there was really no place for her at Rosemont. The boy at the desk was flicking through papers and checking off computerized lists. "Are you sure it's Gardner with a G?" he asked, looking up at her. Jill nodded, too scared to make her voice audible.

What do I do if there's no place for me here? she wondered. She imagined going back to the state university and finding that there was no longer a place for her there, either, desperately calling around to other schools and finding that the only place with an opening was the Pacific Auto Mechanics College. *You're being ridiculous,* she told herself, and at that moment the boy drew out another computerized list. "Ah, here we are. You were on a different list because you were a late admission. Gardner, Jill—your room is over in McGregor, one fourteen. You're going to be rooming with someone called Sheridan Ashley, or maybe it's Ashley Sheridan. Anyway you'll find out soon, I guess. You want someone to show you the way to McGregor?"

"It's OK. I can find it," Jill said, wanting to sound calm and efficient. "I remember it from when I did the tour. Isn't it the old house behind the cafeteria?"

The boy smiled. "Smart girl—always remember where the food is, and you can't go wrong. That's right. You keep on driving out of here, around behind this block, and you'll see the dining room and then McGregor. Good luck. See you later!"

Sandy was on the steps again as Jill and her parents came out. "After you've found your dorm, there's a little reception for parents over in administration—that's the big building with all the ivy. You get a chance to meet the dean and all that."

"I'm glad they've put you here," Jill's mother commented as the car drove past a clump of bushes to park beside the wooden front porch of McGregor. The building was like a huge old, white-painted house, with a front porch draped with wisteria running the length of it.

"Jill, why don't you go up and find your room and we'll start unloading the car," Jill's father suggested as the car ground to a halt on the gravel. "Maybe your roommate is already there, and she can come down to help carry things."

"All right, Daddy," Jill said, trying to sound bright and confident. "I'll be right back." She ran up the three creaking steps and pushed open the front door. It opened right into a lounge area, full of overstuffed chairs and a big brick fireplace at one end. The smell was not damp and musty as that at Hollister, but a pleasant mixure of furniture polish, pine cleaner, and old wood. She stood for a while just inside the front door. The house was completely silent as if she were the first person to come and disturb its long sleep.

She checked out the passageway downstairs first and found it contained rooms one through twenty, then turned up the broad, dark, wood staircase, dimly lit by a diamond-shaped stained-glass window, which threw a rainbow on the worn carpet. One fourteen was almost at the end of the hall. She knocked timidly, then turned the handle. The room inside struck her immediately as cold and brown. The walls were painted off white, but a large brown closet was in the left-hand corner. There were brown book shelves above the beds. The bathroom had a brown door. The two chests and desks were brown, and the beds were covered with thin brown blankets. There were marks on the walls and scratches on the furniture. The floor was covered in dusty speckled tile.

"Oh," she said, feeling a wave of disappointment welling up inside her. She remembered the rooms she had visited the previous fall. They had been bright rooms, full of life and color. There had been bright comforters on the beds, walls covered in pictures, and plants all around.

Jill imagined coming back to this room after a hard day of study, lying on a bed in the middle of unfriendly drabness. She thought back longingly to her room at home—the pretty lace-edged curtains at the window, the white wicker chair with its bright pillows, her stuffed animals sitting in a row along the foot of her bed. Her parents had papered the room, her mother had made the curtains and the pillows. This room was so lonely and so cold and so unfriendly that she almost ran back downstairs and begged to go home again. Instead, she tried to put on a bright face when she met her parents staggering across the front hall with the first load.

"I've found it and it's up here," she called. "Here, let me take that, Mom. It's only up one flight."

"How's the room?" her father asked.

"It's OK," she said.

"Your roommate's not here yet?" her mother asked.

"Nobody's here yet. The whole house seems to be empty."

"That's nice. You get to settle yourself in first," her father said as Jill pushed open the door.

"It's a good thing I don't own too many clothes," Jill commented as her mother helped her hang things in her closet. "They aren't too generous with the closet space."

"Which bed are you taking?" her father asked, staggering in with a heavy box of books and Jill's comforter balanced on top.

"I guess I'd better wait and see how my roommate feels," she said cautiously.

"You're here first," her father said. "First come, first served."

"I don't want to start off with any bad feelings," she said, leaving the comforter on top of the books. She looked around the room. One bed was tucked into a neat little alcove, between the door and the bathroom. The other was fitted in along the window with its chest beside it. Jill thought it would probably be very cold in the winter.

"At least I'll put my ballerina print up," she said, spotting a hook already on the wall. "That will make the place look more cheerful."

"I know we won't recognize it the next time we see it, it will be buried under so many things," her mother said as she unpacked some of Jill's things and put her shoes in a neat row along the closet shelf.

"I hope they have a place in the basement where you can store your boxes and cases, or you'll have to keep climbing over them."

"I guess I'll find that out at the freshman meeting," Jill said.

"This is the last load," her father announced, coming in with the lamp and the stereo. "Where do these go?"

"I'll put them on this desk for now," Jill said. "I hope my roommate hurries up and gets here."

"I'm sure she'll be here soon, darling," her mother said. "Are you going to walk over with us to meet the dean?"

"I think we meet him officially later today," Jill said. "I think I'd better stick around to meet my roommate."

"Then we'd better be going if you want to drop in on the dean, Alice," her father said, looking around with signs of impatience. "Long drive home and Jill's waiting to get settled in, I can tell. I think we should take off now, don't you?"

"Maybe we should get going," her mother said slowly. "Unless you'd like us to stay with you until your roommate gets here, honey."

"Oh, no, I'll be fine, Mom," Jill said brightly. "You want to get back in time for dinner."

"Then we'll be going, Jill," her mother said awkwardly. "Bye, darling. Have a wonderful time, won't you? Enjoy every moment. Make the most of it."

"I will, Mom," Jill said, stepping forward to hug her. "And I won't let strange boys into my room, and I'll brush my teeth . . . ." They both started laughing as they stood with their arms clasped around each other. Then Jill turned to her father. "Bye, Dad," she said softly. He wrapped her into a bear hug, even though he was usually much more comfortable with a handshake.

"Bye, honey," he said. "You take good care of yourself. And if you need us, just call anytime."

"I'll be fine, Daddy," she said.

"Then we'll be going," he said, turning toward the door. "Come on, Alice. Long drive ahead of us."

Jill heard their footsteps move down the hall and heard the car drive away. She walked over to the window and looked out. When the pines moved in the breeze she could see a glint of the river. Her hands felt cold against the wood of the window ledge.

Come back, she felt like yelling. *I do still need you. Don't leave me here alone.*

SIX

Sheridan Ashley arrived just before the freshman meeting was to start. For a long hour Jill had stayed in her room, aware that the house around her was gradually coming to life. She could hear the slam of doors, footsteps on the floor above, and fragments of conversations. Yet when she opened her door and peered out, her own floor was still silent.

She was beginning to think that she would have to go to the meeting alone when she heard the neat tap of heels on the hall and her door flung open. Jill broke into a wide smile. Standing before her was a girl who—at first glance—might have been Toni. She had very wide blue eyes that looked quite surprised. She had blond curls—a lot more tamed than Toni's had ever been. And she couldn't have been more than five feet tall. Her wardrobe, however, was nothing like Toni's. She was wearing very tight black pants, an enormous black sweater, and high spike heels. She glanced around the room in disgust, but her face lit up when she saw Jill.

"Oh, you're Jill," she said breathlessly. "Thank heavens for that. All summer long I wrote to my assigned roommate, and she was great. Then, at the last minute, she decided to spend a year traveling. I was sure my good luck wouldn't last, and I'd end up with a real weirdo. I kept on wondering what I'd do if I got here and found that the room was full of incense and had a tank of piranhas in the corner. All the way up the stairs I kept on chanting to myself, 'Please don't let her be weird; please don't let her be weird.' I guess my prayers were answered. I know we're going to get along fine. I'm Sheridan, by the way, in case they didn't tell you."

Jill smiled. "They weren't sure at the desk if you were Sheridan or Ashley."

"Stupid people," Sheridan said, flinging her garment bag down on the nearest bed. "They always manage to mess things up. They even wrote to me once as 'Dear Mr. Ashley.' My mother had a fit worrying that they had me down as a male and would give me a male roommate. I wouldn't have minded that! Did you just get here?"

"About an hour ago," Jill said. "We have to go down to the freshman meeting in a few minutes. I was worried about going alone."

"I know how you feel," Sheridan said, pulling a brush from her enormous black bag and flicking it through her hair. "Terrifying, isn't it? I almost turned around and went back home again." She threw down her brush onto the nearest chest and looked around the room. "What a dump. I was expecting one of those rooms they showed us on the tour. Still, I bet we can get it fixed up pretty quickly. I brought some of my favorite posters with me. Did you?"

"I brought a few things," Jill said. "I thought I'd wait to see how much space we had."

Sheridan looked around the walls. "Well, we can take down that old picture they've left up for a start," she said, reaching up and taking down Jill's precious ballerina print. "I hate boring walls, don't you? Wait till you see this fantastic fabric graphic I've got. I took it out of our den. My mother doesn't even know I've got it yet! I hope she won't be too mad."

"Where is all your stuff?" Jill asked, wondering if Sheridan's entire college clutter was in her garment bag.

"Here, I hope," Sheridan said. "We shipped it, and it should have arrived a couple of days ago. I'll get someone to help bring it up right after the meeting."

"Speaking of meetings," Jill said, "I think we'd better go, if we don't want to be crammed in at the back."

"OK, Jill," Sheridan said brightly. "You lead the way. I'm going to tag along behind you for the first few days. I can't remember where anything is, and I'm hopeless in new places."

They walked down the stairs and out of McGregor, joining the other people who were making their way toward Hollister.

"I'm glad I wasn't too late," Sheridan confided. "That horrible plane is always delayed, and today it was worse than usual."

"Where did you come from?" Jill asked, feeling rather awed by someone who always took planes.

"San Francisco," Sheridan said. "That's where my mother lives. But I fly up here all the time to be with my father in Portland. We used to live up here until my mother couldn't stand the climate any longer and divorced my father. I don't mind the rain, personally. How about you?"

Jill smiled. "I'm from Seattle, so this will seem dry to me," she said.

Sheridan laughed. "You should see where we live now if you want dry. We're down out of the fog belt, and it doesn't rain for months at a time. All the hills get brown, but it's great if you like swim parties. Personally, I'm not too crazy about them. They make my hair turn green."

"It's funny," Jill said. "When I met my best friend, back in second grade, she had just moved from California and she had green hair. She looks a lot like you, too."

"Is she at school here?" Sheridan asked.

"She's not at school anywhere right now," Jill said. "Her dad had a heart attack, so everything is postponed for her."

"Poor kid," Sheridan said. "I don't think I'd give up my plans because my dad got sick. Neither of my parents has ever given up any plans for me. I couldn't wait to get away from home. I nearly went crazy this summer. My mother is the interfering type, and she doesn't like any of my friends. Are your folks like that?"

"They're kind of overprotective," Jill said, smiling as she thought of them. "But they don't interfere. And they think Toni's wonderful."

"Is that your boyfriend?"

"No, she's my best friend. But they like my boyfriend, too."

"Is he here?" Sheridan asked, looking around as if she expected to see him.

"No, he's a sophomore at State University at Thomson," Jill said.

"So it's going to be long distance romance," Sheridan said thoughtfully. "That's not easy."

"I know," Jill admitted. "But Rosemont was too good a chance to give up."

"What's so special about Rosemont?" Sheridan asked, surprised. "I'd much rather have gone to Berkeley or somewhere bigger. But my mother and her mother came here, so I didn't get much choice."

"Academically it's one of the best," Jill said. "Especially for English, which is going to be my major."

Sheridan eyed her suspiciously. "You're not going to be one of those super brains, are you?" she asked.

"No way," Jill admitted. "I'm going to have to study hard just to keep up here. I'm terrified of being thrown out because I'm not good enough."

"Oh, that's baloney," Sheridan said. "They never throw anyone out of Rosemont. My mother said so. She said once you're in, you're in. Unless you set fire to the dorm or something. I'm certainly not a brain, and I'm not worrying. I plan to have a great time, and I want my roommate to have a great time, too."

"Oh, I intend to," Jill said. "I want to make the most of everything."

Sheridan's eyes glowed. "We'll have such fun together," she said. "I'm glad I've got such a nice roommate."

They walked up the steps together into Hollister.

"Let's sit close to the back," Sheridan suggested as they entered the round room. "Then we can make a quick escape if we want to. These things can get pretty boring."

Jill began to remind Sheridan that the meeting was mandatory, then caught herself. She didn't want Sheridan thinking she was a brain and a goody-goody, too.

"Besides," Sheridan whispered, "I hate sitting in the middle of strange rooms when I don't know anybody." She slid into a chair and pulled Jill down beside her. "Is it just me, or do you think everyone else looks strange?" she asked. Jill looked around the room. She saw lots of kids, some whispering to people next to them, others staring straight to the front, some looking boldly around the room, grinning cheerfully every time they caught somebody's eye. Some were dressed in their best clothes—boys in suits and girls in dresses—others in frayed jeans and battle jackets. Immediately ahead of them were a boy and girl in sweats and headbands, who must have come straight in from jogging. Some boys had long hair spilling over their collars; others looked as if they were about to join the marines.

"What a wild group," she confided to Sheridan. "It's hard to imagine that we're going to know all these people really well one day."

"I don't know if I'd want to know them all really well," Sheridan said, grinning. "Look at that girl with the notepad in her hand. And that boy with the ponytail. I'm glad I'm not his roommate. That T-shirt looks as if it's never been washed. She jumped up in her seat. "Oh, wait a minute—that looks like—it is! Ali, hey, Ali Simons!"

A dark head in the front row turned around, caught sight of Sheridan, and laughed. "Hey, it's Sheridan! You got banished here, too." She turned to her neighbor. "It's Sherry Ashley."

More faces turned toward Sheridan and waved. She waved happily back.

"My dad's neighbors," she confided. "They went to school with me at Columbia Academy before I moved.

"Fran's here, too," the dark girl went on, not seeming to notice that she was speaking over several rows of heads. "But she's late as usual."

"And what about Roger?" Sheridan called back.

"Oh, he went to Princeton. He said he couldn't wait to get far away."

Sheridan laughed. "Sounds like Roger. But I'm mad he's not here. He was fun."

Before Sheridan could discover that she knew the entire freshman class, a door at the front opened and a line of people filed in, a stern-looking man followed by what looked like a collection of faculty members. They talked among themselves as they sat on chairs placed at the front of the room. Sheridan sank back into her chair beside Jill. "Half of Columbia seems to be here," she whispered. "Talk about trying to get away from it all!"

The room grew quiet as the stern man stood and introduced himself as Dr. Pennington, dean of students, and some of the distinguished-looking characters around him as department heads. He gave what must have been his standard welcoming speech to incoming freshmen, speaking of the great opportunities for and still greater responsibilities of the educated human being.

He sounds as if he wants the entire freshman class to win the Nobel peace prize while discovering the cure for cancer, Jill thought. She was about to whisper this to Sheridan but saw that Sheridan was staring intently toward the speaker with a fascinated look on her face. Maybe she was being inspired by this talk, Jill thought.

She stole another glance at Sheridan. It was hard to tell what she was really like. She claimed to be shy, then turned out to know half the freshman class. She wanted to sit near the back to slip out if she got bored, then seemed to be listening more closely than anyone else. *And because she reminds me of Toni, I have to be extra careful,* Jill told herself. *I can't expect her to act like someone else.*

After a long half hour, during which there were many subdued coughs and much scraping of chairs, the dean finished to polite applause, then swept out of the room, followed by the members of the faculty. Sheridan touched Jill's arm. "See that guy sitting way over there on the side. He's really cute, don't you think? I've been trying to get him to notice me. Maybe he thinks freshmen are beneath him!"

After that a large, gray-haired woman got to her feet and introduced herself as Mrs. Grant, the college housing administrator. She introduced the housing office staff and the senior students who would be acting as resident assistants, or R.A.s, in each dorm. "These are the first people you should go to with your problems," she said. "If they can't sort things out, they will find someone who can, whether you have a roommate problem, an academic problem, or a more personal problem."

Then she began to read a list of dormitory rules: no pets in rooms, no music after ten-thirty P.M., no alcohol in the dorms, no cooking in rooms, no smoking in nonsmoking areas. At first Jill tried to take in all the rules, but after page two she was as lost and bored as everyone else. Some of them seemed absolutely meaningless to her: no student shall be admitted to a residence hall without a key card or positive identification by the proctor on duty. The administrator finished her speech by urging everyone to make the most of the freedom college offered.

Before anyone could leave the auditorium, a boy in the front row rose to his feet. "Furthermore," he said in a tone identical to Mrs. Grant's, "breathing will only be allowed on alternate Tuesdays by permission of the proctor, whatever he is!" The whole assembly broke into rowdy laughter.

Jill and Sheridan made their way out of the hall, swept along by the general crush of students.

"Where do we go now?" Sheridan asked.

"Dinner, I think," Jill said. "It's nearly six o'clock."

The crowd was obviously heading for the cafeteria. Jill and Sheridan were about to join the line to pick up their trays when they saw frantic waving from much farther ahead. It was the girls from Sheridan's old school, beckoning madly. "Sherry—up here. We saved you a place!" they yelled.

"Oh, great, I hate lines," Sheridan said. "Come on, Jill."

Jill hung back. "I don't know if I should crash the line, too."

"Of course you should," Sheridan said. "Come on." So Jill followed, red cheeked with embarrassment, as they both moved up the line. Sheridan introduced Jill to her friends, then the little group launched into a discussion of people and places Jill didn't know. As they chattered, Jill fell behind the others and surveyed the array of food on the metal counter in front of her. She was amazed by the huge serving area and the variety of choices. Toni's brother, Will, made endless jokes about dismal college food. He obviously had never been to Rosemont.

Jill helped herself to some salad, then took a plate for the main course. "What's in these?" she asked a girl behind the counter, pointing to an interesting-looking yellow pie.

The girl shrugged her shoulders. "I don't know," she said.

Jill considered taking one when she felt a tap on her shoulder. "If they say they don't know, it means they do know, but they're not telling," a boy behind her whispered. She turned and recognized him as the person at whom Sheridan had been unsuccessfully gazing. He was tall and dark with blue eyes. His short brown hair and scrubbed tan complexion made up the classic good looks Jill and Toni frequently admired as they pored over new catalogs. He smiled at Jill as she looked back at him.

"So you don't advise it?" she asked suspiciously.

He shook his head. "Lesson one in college survival: never eat anything when it's not obvious what it is. Lesson two: never eat anything that is colored yellow. They reserve yellow food coloring for items that would otherwise be totally unappetizing. Hence, you will discover that most of our food is colored yellow here. Seniors actually have yellow tongues."

"So what do you recommend?" Jill asked, not knowing whether she was being teased or not.

"The hamburger," the boy said, taking one himself. "There isn't that much you can do to a hamburger, providing you don't start off with possum meat or something."

"OK. A hamburger, I guess," Jill said, taking one and moving down the line. She paused in front of a dish of deep red Jell-O. "This isn't yellow," she said. "Do you recommend it?"

He shrugged his shoulders. "It's OK if you like beets," he said.

"Beets?" she asked, horrified. "I thought it was raspberry."

"Believe me, beets!" he said. "Skip the Jell-O. Take the ice cream. It comes straight from a carton—and the chocolate sauce comes from a bottle."

"Thanks," Jill said. "You saved me from embarrassing myself at my first college dinner."

"Glad to be of service," he said. "I'll see you around. What dorm do you have?" He made a face when she told him. "Small dorms can be boring," he said. "I'm the third floor R.A. in Phillips. That's the best party dorm. What's your name?"

"Jill Gardner."

"I'm Kyle Robertson," he said. "See ya, Jill." Then he walked away, while Jill followed Sheridan and her friends to a long table.

SEVEN

Dear Toni,

I have now been here almost a week, and I think I'm finally settling in. Everything was so confusing for the first couple of days, but you get to know people really quickly here. I was lucky because my roommate knew a whole bunch of people to start with, so I had a ready-made group. Everybody feels as if we've been here forever, but I think that feeling will probably disappear when the upperclassmen come back and classes start. Until now we have just met with advisers. It's funny really. They show you this huge catalog of courses to choose from and you think, *Wow, how exciting!* Then they tell you that this course is required for freshmen, and it's a good idea to get this one out of the way for your humanities requirement, and by the time they've finished advising, you have no choice at all! I'm taking the development of Western civilization, so anything you need to know about

74

Western civilization from now on, don't be afraid to ask!

Jill put down her pen and smiled as she imagined Toni reading the letter. The wind blustered outside, and the pine trees sighed and groaned. Jill could almost hear Toni's voice: "OK, so you're taking a few courses, but what about the good stuff? Have you met any cute guys yet? What about your roommate and parties?"

The other thing we've been doing all week is going to endless parties. Every club and society in college is trying to snap up all the freshmen. Some of them sound like fun, but I'm scared of committing myself to anything before I see how tough the work is going to be. Sheridan, my roommate, has signed up for almost everything. She joined the debating club, because she says she's good at fighting with her mother, and the tennis team, because she's always played at her country club. I think she's even signed up for soccer, because it's a good way to meet boys! I don't know how she'll have any time left for classes, but she doesn't seem to care!

She's the sort of person who has only come to college for four years to have fun and meet boys—sounds like you, doesn't she? In a way she is. She looks a lot like you, but I have to keep remembering that she's not you. When her stuff finally arrived the first evening—she had flown up from San Francisco—she asked me to put her shoes on the top shelf because she couldn't reach it. I can never remember anything being out of your reach, Toni, even if you have to balance telephone books on a chair to get to it.

I have to remember that she doesn't have your sense of humor, either. The other day she said she wished her hair would hurry up and grow. Without thinking I told her that she could hang by her hair from the light fixture to stretch it—do you remember telling me that once back in elementary school? You told me it was an ancient secret of the Egyptians, and you said it so seriously that I almost believed you. Anyway, she gave me this look as if I was crazy, and I had to tell her that it was an old joke between Toni and me.

Apart from little things like that, everything is fine. She is nice to me, and we are getting along well. She's so happy to get away from her mother, who she says is very domineering and tries to run her life. That was how she got me as a roommate. Sherry's mother made her put that her interests were reading and writing, so that she'd get a studious roommate! Sheridan wanted to put rock music and parties, but her mother filled in the form and mailed it first. As it turns out, we like enough of the same things. It just takes getting used to, sharing a room with somebody when you have had your own room all your life.

Jill stared out the window again. Outside the light was fading—the sky behind the pine trees was tinged with pink as the sun went down behind the river. She tried not to be annoyed by Sheridan. After all, she was used to having things her own way. Sheridan was trying to be nice. She just didn't realize when she had stepped on somebody's toes. She hadn't even realized the ballerina print was Jill's when she took it down. The big red, black, and white graphic print she had hung in its place was much brighter. It just wasn't the sort of thing Jill liked very much.

It had been the same way with the bed. "Do you mind very much if I have this bed?" she had asked Jill, lifting Jill's comforter from the bed in the alcove. "I get terrible allergies if I sleep near a window, and I really don't want to keep you awake coughing and wheezing all night." Jill could hardly say no to that, so she now had the bed by the window while Sheridan was tucked up snugly in the alcove.

"But we are both trying hard to be considerate right now," Jill continued writing.

I've let her have most of the closet space because she has hundreds more clothes than I do, and she plays her stereo with the headphones on. You should see her stereo, Toni. It has everything built in—speakers, turntable, twin tape deck, radio. It looks as if it could direct a space flight singlehandedly. You should hear the amount of noise it can give out if you don't use the headphones! Sheridan seems to know half the freshman class, and they always drop in after meals. They seem to enjoy talking over a billion decibels of sound. Maybe by the end of the year I'll enjoy my music that way.

Actually Sherry might not own her stereo by the end of the year. She has already been warned twice by the resident assistant (R.A.) about having the volume too high. She doesn't seem to go for rules much.

But I seem to be the only freshman who really worries about the rules. They told us there was to be no noise after ten-thirty and no alcohol in the rooms. Well, that very evening after dinner, someone said, 'Hey, let's have a party!' and before you knew it there were a hundred people in our room, plus a beer keg and a lot of noise. I went along because I didn't want to be classed as a weirdo, but I stuck to soda all evening. Some of the kids got really noisy and rushed up and down the halls screaming. I went to bed around midnight when the party moved to another floor, but Sherry said it lasted until six A.M.

I guess people will have to keep more reasonable hours once the professors start piling on the work. I meet my English department adviser Monday! Wish me luck. I hope he likes me, since we are going to have to see each other regularly for the next four years. Four years seem like a long time right now, but Kyle says it goes quickly. He is a senior R.A. in another dorm, and I have seen him twice in the cafeteria. Sheridan is very mad because he talks to me and not her. She's chasing him like crazy, but he doesn't seem to notice. Maybe he talked to me because I'm not chasing him. He has done me an enormous service already by warning me what not to eat! They have a talent for making the weirdest things look good as they sit up on the counter.

Oh, here's Sheridan back—loud giggles are approaching down the hall. I'd better finish this for now. Write back, or else! I've got to write to Craig tonight, too. I haven't even written to him yet, so you are honored. Hope your dad is much better.

Love, Jill.
P.S. Please write back soon.

Jill finished the letter, folded it, and put it into an envelope. "I hope that letter doesn't sound too homesick," she said to herself as she shook her wrist out. She took a deep breath as the door opened, and a crowd of laughing students burst in.

EIGHT

"Are you with us, Miss Gardner?" Dr. Holloman asked in his clipped voice.

Jill jumped, blushed scarlet, and turned her gaze away from the window.

"I'm sorry, Dr. Holloman," she muttered. "I really was listening."

"I realize that a rose garden is slightly more desirable to look at than my face," he went on, getting a nervous giggle from some of the other students. "But anyone who does not pay attention to everything I am about to say will find himself with an F on his first paper."

Jill gulped and stared down at her notebook. Of all the people to offend in college! She wanted so much to do well in English. But Dr. Holloman seemed as if he would be the hardest of her instructors to please. She had dreamed of a kindly old English professor who rambled on about the romantic poets. Instead she got this tall, thin, man with rimless spectacles and a balding head above a young-looking face. He had a habit of staring over the top of those rimless spectacles that Jill found very unnerving. Equally unnerving was his habit of flinging out questions at the class, then yelling, "Wrong!" in great delight as the students stammered answers.

This was only their second meeting and already Jill had angered him. *Why did Holloman walk by the one time I glanced out of the window?* she thought angrily as she scribbled down headings from the blackboard.

Her gaze had wandered for only a few seconds as she thought about Sheridan. *Why can't I stop thinking about her?* Jill questioned herself.

Jill was starting to make her second trip to the laundry room early that morning, when Sheridan had emerged from the bathroom. Her head was wrapped in a huge pink towel, and she squeaked with delight when she saw Jill's arms full of clothes.

"Oh, are you heading for the laundry room? Would you be an angel and throw in a few things of mine? You know how claustrophobic I am. I just can't stand it down there in the basement!"

Then she picked up piles of dirty clothes from the floor and balanced them on top of Jill's pile, without waiting for an answer. Jill had not said anything. She had gone down to the basement and washed Sheridan's clothes as well as her own. But she quietly grew angry.

I suppose I can understand how she feels, Jill had thought as she stood in the steamy half darkness listening to the creak and plop of the washing machine. *It's not too pleasant down here. But I don't want to be stuck with doing her washing all year.* Then she thought of the piles of dirty clothes that Sheridan never picked up. *On the other hand,* she decided, *maybe I'd rather wash her things myself than have to put up with that mess!*

When she had returned Sheridan seemed grateful. "You are so wonderful," she said. "I don't know how you can stand it down there. I took one look at it and I knew that I could never face it again."

Jill sighed as she tried to turn her full attention to Dr. Holloman.

"The subject is of your choosing," he was saying. "I really want to see whether any of you can write grammatically correct English. And just let me mention that no student belongs at Rosemont if he is not completely familiar with the spelling and grammar rules of the English language. Papers with grammatical errors find their way straight into my wastebasket."

The boy beside Jill glanced nervously in her direction. Jill made an attempt at a smile.

"Having got that out of the way," Dr. Holloman continued, "let me give you your reading list for this semester." He began handing out a mimeographed list of titles and authors. Without even counting, Jill could see that the list contained at least a dozen books. They were all novels she was longing to read, but even as she thought about discussing Jane Austen and Charlotte Bronte with Dr. Holloman, she could feel her stomach tightening into a knot. She had already been to the college bookstore for history and psychology textbooks. One of the students standing in line next to her had muttered under his breath, "You can decide if you want *Abnormal Behavior* or a new Porsche!" Jill had laughed. Some of the students could own new Porsches if they wanted to, but Jill was painfully aware of how much Rosemont was costing her parents, and she didn't want to have to ask for a penny extra all year. Yet she had already spent more than half her book allowance, and the year was barely a week old.

At the end of the class she approached Dr. Holloman's desk. "Excuse me, Dr. Holloman," she began. "Is it necessary to purchase all these books, or are they available in the library?"

"Necessary?" he said, slamming a book shut so violently that Jill almost dropped the ones she was carrying. "Of course it is not necessary. You can go and spend your money on Harlequin novels for all I care. You can get a job in a five-and-dime store without buying any of these books. You can raise ten children without buying any of these books. But if you want to pass my class, Miss Gardner, you are well advised to read and study and know each of these works. I don't believe that can be done by checking them out of the library for a week."

"Yes, Dr. Holloman," Jill stammered. She fled from the classroom back to the dorm.

As she opened the door to her room, a great burst of laughter met her. Nine or ten pairs of eyes turned in her direction.

"Oh, hi, Jill," Sheridan said. "Peter was just telling us about when his dad was at Rosemont."

Jill picked her way across the room, stepping over Sheridan's jeans, people's legs, piles of books, and half-empty Coke cans. She pushed aside Sheridan's hairbrush and curlers to put her books down on her desk. Her face still burned with embarrassment, and she wanted to be alone. But she couldn't ask Sheridan to take her friends and leave her own room.

A boy named Ray leaned across and opened the refrigerator. "Here, grab a Coke," he said, throwing her one expertly. "Scoot over and make room for her, Ali."

Ali gave Jill a half smile and moved over a few inches. Jill opened the Coke and sat on her own bed between Ali and Angela.

"So how come Rosemont was so much fun in those days, that's what I want to know?" Sheridan demanded. "Up till now it's been boring, boring, boring."

Ali stretched like a cat. "Oh, I don't know if flying underwear from a flagpole is so wildly exciting," she said.

"Oh, come on," Peter said, looking up from his corner on the floor. "Where's your sense of adventure? That's what you go to college for—to do all the wild things you could never do anywhere else. Why don't we do something crazy?"

"Like what?" Ali demanded.

"Like fill the swimming pool with ice cream and see if we can swim in it?" Peter suggested. Everyone laughed.

"What a way to drown, in strawberry ice cream!" Sheridan squealed.

"Don't talk about ice cream," Ali said, sighing. "I'm starving. Have you guys got anything to eat in here?"

"I think I saw some yogurt in the fridge," Sheridan said, opening it up and taking out a container.

Jill just stopped herself from saying, "But that's my yogurt." That would have sounded too petty. Instead she said, "Leave one of those yogurts for me tonight, will you? I'll need a snack while I'm working on my paper."

Sheridan peered into the fridge. "Sorry, this is the last one," she said.

"But I bought three yesterday," Jill blurted out. "What happened to them?"

Sheridan looked at Jill as if she were speaking Chinese. "Well, I ate them, of course," she said. "What did you think—a burglar broke in here just to get your crummy yogurt?"

The others laughed, and Jill pretended to laugh, too. "It's OK," she said. "I just need a snack for tonight."

Again Sheridan looked at her as if she weren't right in the head. "The stores are open all afternoon. You can go buy another one," she said.

Jill looked around the room. She realized that none of the people would worry about the price of yogurt. *I've got to stop worrying if I want to fit in here*, she told herself. *I've got to join in and do the things other people do. I'm just too used to living in a very quiet, very organized house* .

It was a mistake to think of home. As she thought the words, a picture of her kitchen at home flashed into her mind, her mother tipping out a fresh batch of cookies as she and Toni came in from school.

"Those cookies smell so good, Mrs. Gardner," Toni was saying. "If they ever invent smellyvision, I'll nominate you for a cooking show."

Jill's mother laughed. "Why, thank you, Toni. Would you like one? Watch out, though, the chocolate is still hot."

"I'm suppose to be on a diet," Toni said. "But I can't resist." Then she popped the cookie into her mouth. Jill sighed to herself as she thought of that scene. Even Toni, who was like another daughter in the Gardners' house, never took things without asking. *Why does everyone I love have to be so far away?* Jill wondered.

"What's wrong, Jill?" Peter asked.

"Nothing," she said. "Does anyone else feel homesick? Sometimes it just hits me that I'm so far away from home."

Sheridan laughed. "Homesickness is something I'll never suffer from as long as I live," she said. "I couldn't wait to get away."

"Me, neither," Ali agreed.

"And I've been away at school for four years," Peter said. "Nobody's ever home anyway."

"Cheer up, you'll get over it," Angela said. "I know—why don't we order out to Weird Willies for pizza instead of going over to the cafeteria for lunch. That'll make us all feel good."

"Great idea," Peter said, leaping up. "What's the number? How many large pizzas can ten of us eat?"

"How about ten?" Ray asked, laughing.

Peter went down the hall to order, leaving Jill feeling worried again. This pizza business was becoming an expensive daily habit. But Jill knew she could hardly leave and go to the cafeteria without everyone thinking she was unfriendly. So she put in her three dollars with everyone else's and ate a couple of pieces of pizza.

After lunch the group began to gather their possessions and leave.

"Anyone feel like going dancing tonight?" Ali asked. "I still haven't tried that place in town."

"Magoos or Magees or whatever?" Ray asked. "Yeah, they say it's pretty good. Let's go."

"But I've got nothing to wear for dancing," Sheridan moaned.

Ali laughed. "You always say that, and I don't know anybody who has more clothes!"

"But nothing that looks right," Sheridan said. "Maybe I'll have time to go out and buy something this afternoon. You want to come with me, Jill?"

"Not today, Sheridan," Jill said. "I have my first English paper to work on. I'm going to the library."

"But the semester just started," Angela said, looking horrified. "You don't have to get down to serious stuff this early!"

"You don't have my English teacher," Jill said. "He's going to be very picky, and I really want to do well in his class."

Jill saw a couple of the kids look at each other.

"Anyone would think college was for studying or something," Peter said, laughing. "Come on, you guys. Does anyone have a class this afternoon?"

The room gradually emptied, and Jill hurried to the library. She wanted to do a paper that would make Dr. Holloman realize she was not an unintelligent person who only stared out of windows. She worked without stopping for dinner and finally returned to her room, tired but satisfied, around nine.

At least Sheridan is out dancing tonight, she thought. She let herself in and stood there in the half darkness, enjoying the peace of being alone. She was walking across to her bed when she stumbled over something on the floor.

Jill bent to pick up the piece of clothing. She reached across to her desk and turned on her lamp to see if the item needed to be hung up or put into the laundry bag. She froze as she saw what it was. "Oh, no," she muttered. "Oh, no."

She was holding her own white lace blouse. As she turned it over, she saw that there was now an ugly brown stain down the front. For a while she stood there, paralyzed. Then the tears began to well up, and before she could stop them, they streamed down her cheeks.

Jill walked over to the bed and lay down, still clutching the blouse. She was unsure how much time had passed when she was awakened by the sound of Sheridan's key in the lock.

"Why, Jill," Sheridan said as she entered. "What's the matter? Is something wrong?"

Jill nodded, looking up at Sheridan with puffy, red eyes.

"Are you sick?" Sheridan asked. "Do you want me to call a doctor?"

"I don't need a doctor," Jill said in a broken voice. "A doctor couldn't do anything about this." She held up the blouse for Sheridan to see.

Sheridan flushed. "Look, I'm really sorry about that," she said. "We were drinking coffee before we went out, and Peter and Jonas started playing football, and they knocked my arm while I had a cup of coffee in my hand. I was really mad at them."

"But you wore my blouse without asking me," Jill stammered. "You had no right to do that."

"Well, my red blouse was dirty, so I thought white would go with these black pants. You weren't anywhere around to ask, but I didn't think you'd mind."

"You didn't think I'd mind?" Jill shrieked. "Sheridan, that was my very best blouse. I'd never even worn it. I was saving it for a really special occasion."

Sheridan shrugged her shoulders. "How was I to know that? I said I was sorry," she said. "I'll take it to be cleaned for you tomorrow."

Jill turned away. "There's no way they can get out a coffee stain like that, and you know it. It's ruined."

Sheridan walked past her and flung herself down into the chair. "Look, there's no need to get hysterical over a dumb blouse," she said. "So I'll buy you another one."

"You can't buy me another one," Jill said hopelessly. "I bought this in France. It was a special memory for me. You can never replace it."

"Well, if I'd known it was like the crown jewels or something, I'd never have touched it," Sheridan said. "Honestly, Jill, you do make a fuss about things. You ought to get out and enjoy yourself more. Then little things like blouses wouldn't matter so much to you. Now why don't you get into bed? You'll feel better in the morning."

Jill didn't say any more. She undressed mechanically, folding her clothes neatly at the end of her bed. Then she climbed in between the covers. Although she tried hard to fall asleep, a picture kept creeping into her mind, a picture of the little boutique up on Montmartre and the blouse hanging in the window.

"Go ahead and get it," Toni was saying. "It looks wonderful on you!"

"But all that money, Toni," Jill argued. "And it's so impractical. When would I ever wear a lace blouse?"

"Christopher Columbus made it across to America," Toni had said, giving Jill a teasing smile. "Maybe more Italians might decide to follow him. You want to be prepared for special things to happen in your life, don't you?"

Special things, Jill thought with a big sigh, feeling the cold sheet against her bare toes. *I thought Rosemont would be full of special things. Maybe I don't belong here at all. I wish you were here, Toni. I was trying to be mature and get along with Sheridan, but I don't think I can face a year of this!*

NINE

The next morning there was an uneasy peace between the two girls. Sheridan tried to be nice to Jill, even offering her the bathroom first, which was something she had never done before. Jill tried to answer questions politely, pretending that everything was going to be fine.

How can I go on like this all year? she thought as she walked alone to breakfast. *She's trying to be nice now, but tomorrow she'll only borrow something else or find something else to laugh about with her friends.* The year seemed to stretch out endlessly in front of Jill, with no place to call her own, no one to call her friend, surrounded by people she didn't like. *If only I'd gone to State U. after all*, she thought. *That was the place I was supposed to go to. Not here. I knew I didn't really belong here. If I were at State U. I'd have Craig close by and maybe Toni next year. Now I have nobody.*

All through breakfast she found herself thinking about Toni, wondering what she was doing, whether she had signed up for college yet or found a job. Jill didn't dare hope for a letter yet from her friend. The entire time they were in Europe, Toni managed to write only one postcard to her mother and father.

Jill was gathering her books for a nine o'clock class when she heard her name being called down the hall.

"I thought Rosemont was supposed to be a high-class establishment" were the first words she heard when she picked up the phone. "That yell sounded as if it came from the Seattle docks!"

"Toni!" Jill exclaimed in delight. "It's so good to hear you!"

"I thought you might have forgotten who I was by now," Toni quipped. "What with the pace of the social life at Rosemont. I got your letter, and I knew there was no way I was going to sit down and write, so I thought I'd better phone. How are you doing, Jill?"

"Oh, I'm just fine," Jill said. "Classes have started. In fact, I have to go to my Western civ. class in a few minutes. But that professor is very absentminded. He won't even notice if I'm late. He just talks into the air, and we just take notes. I think he'd go on with the same spiel even if no students showed up. Unlike my English teacher, who throws out horrible questions at us all the time—really terrible questions that make us make judgments, like whether a person was justified in murdering a tyrant. I've just done my first paper for him, and I have to go and discuss it with him next week. I'm in a panic about that already."

"So how's the famous Sheridan?" Toni asked.

"She's fine, I guess," Jill said. "But tell me all about you—I'm dying to know how things are going. How is your dad?"

"Much better," Toni said. "He's out of the hospital. We've got a bed in the den downstairs for him so he doesn't have to climb any stairs. Of course he's still pretty weak, but maybe now that he's back home we can start getting him strong again. I'm so glad he's home, Jill."

"I'm really glad to hear about your father, Toni," Jill said. "What about you? Have you thought about college yet? or getting a job?"

"I really haven't had time to think about myself yet," Toni said. "I feel as if I've been holding my breath and I can't start breathing again until Dad is officially back to his old self. But I've got to start getting back into things pretty soon."

"I'm glad things are starting to get better, anyway," Jill said. "I've been worrying about you."

"And I've been worrying about you, too," Toni said. "So tell me about your friends. Have you met anyone who's as witty and intelligent and fun as me yet?"

"Not yet," Jill said, laughing.

"So what about Sheridan? She didn't turn out to be a best friend yet? You thought she was a lot like me."

"Only to look at," Jill said. "Otherwise she's not like you at all."

"So you don't get along too well?"

"It's OK. Things will sort themselves out, I'm sure. You know what it's like when you try to share a room for the first time. Oh, gosh, Toni. Look at the time. I have to get to my first class, and I'd better not run up your phone bill too much. But I'm really glad you called me. It's so good to hear your voice. I'm in the middle of another long letter to you. I'll try to finish it this weekend. Bye!"

Jill looked longingly at the phone as she put it back on its hook. She wanted to tell Toni everything she'd been feeling, but the hallway in the dorm was no place to pour out her troubles. Besides, Toni had enough troubles of her own.

On Saturday morning Jill watched, a little enviously, as several cars roared off over the gravel and students called out, "Have a good weekend. See you Monday!"

She was not looking forward to a whole weekend with no plans. After almost two weeks of endless parties, none of the clubs had scheduled anything for that weekend. She hoped that Sheridan and her group would not want to party in their room all weekend.

Then, as Jill was walking back from breakfast, she heard a loud yell, which caused her to turn and stare. There was Toni running across the grass toward her.

"What are you doing here?" Jill screamed in delight as she ran toward her friend.

"Is that any way to greet somebody who has just driven a strange car down a strange highway just for you?" Toni asked, laughing as Jill hugged her. "Actually I managed to get my hands on my brother's car, and I was really missing you last week, so I thought, 'Why not? I might as well go see how the other half lives.' I'm starving, by the way. I skipped breakfast to get an early start."

"You're too late for breakfast in the cafeteria, I'm afraid," Jill said. "But you didn't miss much."

"Was the caviar slightly too warm, or the eggs Benedict slightly too cold?" Toni asked teasingly.

"Have you ever had pancakes that bounce?" Jill asked dryly. "I wisely stuck to the fruit and cereal! But come on back to my room and I'll make you some coffee."

"Have you used your corn popper for heating soup yet?" Toni wanted to know as the pair made their way through the fallen leaves.

"I haven't had a chance," Jill said. "It's on duty full-time popping corn. We go through a cornfield a day."

"Boy, you really do entertain on a big scale," Toni said.

"Not me. Sheridan entertains on a big scale."

"Then tell her to get her own corn popper," Toni said.

"Sheridan is not the easiest person to tell things to," Jill said. "She sulks or she makes fun of you to her friends."

"I think this Sheridan person needs telling a thing or two," Toni said.

Jill opened the big front door to McGregor. "Now, Toni," she said, "promise me you won't stir things up. Remember, I have to live here until next June. I don't want a lot of enemies."

"You know me," Toni said, glancing back at Jill as she walked across the front hall. "I am always the most diplomatic person in the world."

"Ha!" Jill said, laughing as the girls climbed the staircase. She realized that it was the first time she had laughed for days. It felt good.

She opened the door cautiously and peeped in. "We're in luck," she said. "Sheridan's not here. She must have gone out for breakfast again. Come on in."

Toni followed her into the room. "Boy, this looks as messy as mine," she said, looking from the unmade bed to the clothing on the floor and the piles of papers. "I never thought I'd see the day when your room looked like this. I guess this is what going away from home does to you!"

"I've sort of given up," Jill said, bending to pick up clothes and papers as she spoke. "The first few days I tried keeping things neat, but stuff just gets thrown on the floor faster than I can pick up."

"Then tell the slob to pick up her own things," Toni said angrily. "You know you don't like living in a mess like this."

Jill shrugged her shoulders, turning away from Toni to put the paper on Sheridan's already overflowing desk. "I guess I must be weird," she said. "Everyone else's room looks a lot like this one."

Toni walked across to the window, then opened the door to her right. "And you even have your own bathroom. Boy, what luxury!" she said, walking in.

From inside came a scream.

"I'm sorry. I didn't realize the room was occupied!" Toni said quickly.

Sheridan's voice shrieked, "Get out of here!" Her cry was followed by a stumbling noise, then a crash and a terrible wail.

Jill could stand it no longer. She rushed into the bathroom. Sheridan's head, wrapped in a bright red bath cap, appeared above a mountain of bubbles in the tub. Her face, twisted with rage, was almost purple. Toni stood trying to look embarrassed and not laugh, while Sheridan spluttered in the bath.

"I'm sorry, really I am," she said. "I had no idea anyone was in here. You know you shouldn't balance things on the edge of the tub like that. They can get knocked over so easily." She turned to Jill. "I sort of knocked over her bubble bath as I was trying to make a dignified exit," she said.

"It was my expensive French bubble bath," Sheridan shouted. "This moron has knocked over my twenty-dollar bubble bath! What's she doing in my room, anyway?"

"Sheridan, this is my friend Toni," Jill said. "You know, the one from Seattle. I've told you about her."

"More than once," Sheridan said, scowling. "Now will you kindly get her out of my bathroom."

Toni looked down seriously at Sheridan. "Did you know you look exactly like a strawberry sundae with a cherry on top?" she asked. Sheridan spluttered through her mountain of pink bubbles. "Get out of here," she yelled. The two girls shut the door, grins spreading across both their faces.

"Not the friendliest person, is she?" Toni asked as they sat down uneasily and Jill plugged in the coffeepot.

"You caught her at a bad moment," Jill said. "And I don't think you improved her mood by knocking over that bubble bath. Honestly, Toni, you are a walking accident."

Toni looked hurt. "I was just trying to get out in a hurry," she said. "There's not much room to turn around in there, and that stupid bottle was perched right on the edge."

At that moment Sheridan appeared, wearing a purple bathrobe, her head wrapped in a purple towel. "You might have warned me that we were about to have a visitor, Jill," she said.

"I'm sorry," Jill muttered. "I didn't know she was coming. It was a surprise visit."

"Yes," Toni said, eyeing Sheridan as if she were a cockroach. "I decided to come down and check on her. She didn't sound too happy when I called her, and I can see why."

"Toni!" Jill began, frowning at her friend.

"Well, I can see why you're unhappy," Toni said. "This doesn't look like your room at all. You don't like living in a mess. You hate things like that disgusting painting on the wall. Where are your posters?"

"Sheridan wanted to brighten up the room," Jill said. "Anyway, let's forget it. I'll pour us some coffee."

"Couldn't you go someplace else?" Sheridan demanded. "I want to get dressed and then my friends are coming over."

"Well, I guess," Jill began, but Toni grabbed her arm.

"This is your room, too, Jill," she said.

"But there are only two of you," Sheridan said in a hurt voice. "You could go down to the coffee shop together. There'll be a whole big group of us."

Toni eyed Sheridan firmly. "We're not going anywhere," she said. She turned to Jill, who was embarrassed. "You have every right to have friends over," she said. She turned back to Sheridan. "This is supposed to be a room that you share. It doesn't seem to me that anyone taught you about sharing way back in kindergarten. This isn't Jill's room at all. These are your things all over the walls, your clothes taking up all the closet. Jill wouldn't say anything because she's too nice and she hates to hurt people's feelings. But I'm not like that. I say what I think. And I think it's about time she felt at home in her own room. You can get dressed in the bathroom, Sheridan, and then you can go someplace else with your friends."

Sheridan's eyes turned steel gray. "I've had just about enough of this, Jill" she said in a hard voice. "Ever since you got here you've been a big pain. You've done nothing but complain about every-thing—including every little sip I take of your crummy cola. You nearly went crazy over that dumb blouse. You're a big drag—you sit there like a wet blanket while my friends and I are trying to have a good time. And the only thing I hear all day is Toni, Toni, Toni! And quite frankly, now that I've met Toni, I don't think much of your taste."

Jill jumped to her feet. "You can say what you like about me, Sheridan Ashley, but don't you insult my friends," she said angrily. "I don't think much of your taste, either, but I've been trying to make the best of it. I know you think you're wonderful, but, to be honest, you are not the easiest person in the world to live with. You think you're the only person in the world who matters. No wonder you didn't want to hear about Toni. I bet you've never had a real friend, treating people the way you do!"

Sheridan looked as if she had been slapped across the face. "How dare you," she yelled. "I'm going to the R.A. right now and demand another roommate. There is no way I can spend another day with you!"

"No, wait," Jill said, fighting down her sudden panic. But Toni stepped in front of her.

"That will suit Jill fine. How soon can you have your stuff moved out?" she asked.

Sheridan eyed Toni coldly. "Me? I'm not going anywhere. It will just be a matter of seeing which of my friends wants to move in with me. Who could possibly want her?" she said, indicating Jill with a flick of her head. She grabbed clothing from her closet, then swept back into the bathroom again.

Jill sank down, white-faced, onto a chair. "Oh, Toni," she whispered. "This is terrible. What have we done?"

"Got you free of the world's worst roommate," Toni said. "Now you can start enjoying college, instead of walking around looking miserable all the time."

"But I won't ever have any friends," Jill said. "Word will get around that I'm a troublemaker. Everyone knows Sheridan. They'll all believe her, and nobody will want to room with me."

Toni grinned. "Let's put it this way," she said. "At the worst you have no roommate at all. Who would you rather room with—Sheridan or nobody?"

Jill got up and pushed back her hair. "If you put it that way," she said with a weak smile, "nobody, I guess."

TEN

The two girls sipped coffee while Sheridan was down in the R.A.'s room. Jill could hardly swallow a sip. She imagined her R.A. regarding her with disgust after hearing Sheridan's story.

Sheridan said little when she returned. "The R.A. says we should try to work it out," she informed Jill stiffly. "I told her there was no way I could work it out, so she said I'd have to wait and see the housing officer on Monday."

Jill stared into her coffee.

Sheridan said nothing more but began to put makeup into a big tote bag. "I'll be over at Ali's," she said as she turned toward the door. "You might start thinking about whom you're going to room with and start packing your stuff."

"I'll wait until we've seen the housing officer," Jill said, trying to stop the sinking feeling in her stomach.

"Come on," Toni said brightly when Sheridan was gone. "I've come all this way, so you might at least give me the grand tour of the campus."

Jill smiled. "You know Toni, I can't keep calling you to come and solve my problems. I'm supposed to be a big girl now."

"Are you trying to say you're not grateful to me for getting rid of the terrible Sheridan?" Toni sounded hurt.

"Of course I'm grateful, you dope," Jill said. "But one of the things that's worrying me is that I was trying hard to handle this problem like a mature adult. And now you appear and in a few seconds of screaming and yelling, the whole thing gets settled. It doesn't seem right, does it?"

Toni grinned and walked down the hall ahead of Jill. "I always find that yelling and screaming get things done better than being polite!" she said.

"But we're supposed to act like grown-ups now. We should talk out our problems," Jill said.

Toni shook her head and stopped walking to face her friend. "That only works if both sides are grown-up," she said. "You were trying to act like an adult, but Sheridan was acting like a kindergartner, yelling, 'Mine, mine, mine' all the time. Thank heavens I showed up when I did. I think you would have cracked soon."

"But you can't go on solving my problems for me, Toni," Jill said. "From now on, let me make my own mistakes, OK? Even if you see that they're going to be mistakes. And I'll do the same for you.

We've got to learn to stand on our own feet, without each other."

"OK," Toni said. "I'll get a phone call from you saying, 'Help, I'm stuck in quicksand,' and I won't come, right?"

Before Jill could answer, a door at the far end of the hall opened, and a girl came out. Jill gripped Toni's arm.

"That's Ali Simons, Sheridan's friend, coming toward us. I bet Sheridan went to her room."

"So what?" Toni said. "What can she do to you?"

"You know I hate being on the wrong side of people," Jill said.

"You can't go through life being everybody's friend," Toni said. "There are bound to be some people you clash with. You've fought with me enough times."

"Only friendly fights," Jill said.

Toni laughed. "They were not friendly at the time. Remember that collision when we were roller-skating waitresses? That was a fight to the death." She wanted Jill to laugh, too, but Jill walked along, tight-lipped, hearing Ali's heels tap down the hall toward them. They met as Jill and Toni started to go downstairs.

"So you and Sherry had a big fight," she said, giving Jill a knowing look. "And now she doesn't want to room with you anymore."

"That's right," Jill said. "I suppose one of you will be moving in instead of me."

Ali shot Jill a horrified look. "Just as long as it's not me!" she said. "I mean, Sheridan's fine to have as a friend, but I wouldn't want to live with her. She'd drive me crazy. Frankly, I wonder you've stuck it out this long. Between you and me, she always was a spoiled little darling. Right now she's busy having hysterics. See you, Jill." She waved and walked on.

Jill looked after her in amazment.

"What did I tell you?" Toni whispered as Ali turned down the hall. "You see—your fairy godmother Toni has made everything all right. You'll get a nice new roommate, and everything will just get better and better."

"Oh, I hope you're right," Jill said. "Being on your own for the first time is so scary sometimes, Toni. Everything is new all at once."

"We felt the same at the beginning of high school," Toni said as they walked out the front door of McGregor and across the gravel driveway. "You said that you'd never find your way around the building and that you wanted to tie a string to the restrooms, so you could get back when you needed them!"

"Toni Redmond, I did not!" Jill said. "You exaggerate. If I remember correctly, you were the one who got lost and ended up in the boys' wrestling portable when you should have been in geography."

A big smile spread across Toni's face. "That was deliberate," she said. "The boys' wrestling team was so much more interesting than a map of Europe!"

"You have always had a one-track mind," Jill said. "This must be the longest you've gone without a boyfriend since the fifth grade."

"I intend to make up for lost time as soon as I start college and get a job," Toni said, grinning wickedly. "Want to make a bet about twenty boys in one semester?"

She strode ahead of Jill toward the main building. She was halfway across the road when two black forms roared up behind them, screeching past in a shower of gravel. Jill screamed as Toni almost stumbled into one of the motorbikes, but the riders didn't stop until they swerved to a violent halt beside the steps.

"What was that?" Toni asked shakily.

Jill glanced over at the bikers and frowned. "It's the craze on campus right now," she said.

"What brainless jerks," Toni began. Then she stopped and clutched Jill's arm. "But certainly cute," she whispered. "Who is he? Do you know him?"

Jill smiled. "As a matter of fact, I do," she said. "He's the famous Kyle I told you about. The one that Sherry was chasing madly and who spoke to me instead. I haven't seen him since the upperclassmen came back."

"Well, introduce me," Toni whispered. "I'll even forgive him for almost running me down. He's gorgeous."

"You're not allowed to come on my campus and steal men," Jill said.

"But I saved you from a fate worse than death with Sheridan," Toni pleaded.

Jill shrugged her shoulders. "Oh, OK," she said. "I'll introduce you."

She felt a warm glow of pride that she actually knew the good-looking upperclassman. They drew level with the two bikers.

"Hi, Kyle," Jill said.

The boy turned and stared at her blankly. "Hi, er—" he said.

"Jill," she reminded him. "You remember, we met in the cafeteria the first day? You warned me about the beet Jell-O?"

"Oh, yeah, sure," he said easily. Although Jill was sure that he didn't remember at all. "How's it going—Jean?" he asked, already moving off again.

"Fine," Jill said, her face hot.

"Looks like you remembered him better than he remembered you," Toni commented dryly.

"I feel like a fool," Jill said.

"Don't be ridiculous," Toni said. "He's obviously one of those jerks who only remember people when it suits him. Now that the upper-classmen are back, he doesn't need to remember a little freshman girl."

"Creep," Jill muttered. Toni laughed. "Don't worry about it. Craig's much cuter than he is. You should bring him down soon. Then you can walk him around and show him off, and everyone will be envious."

Jill sighed. "That'll be nice," she said. "But I don't know when it will happen. Every time I've called him he was so busy. We've had about ten minutes of conversation—all with Quiet Riot blaring in the background, too."

"I'll call him and tell him to pay more attention to you," Toni began.

"Toni—you promised you wouldn't interfere in my life!" Jill started, then saw that Toni was grinning. "And will you stop teasing me?" she asked.

"I just wanted you to smile," Toni said. "This morning you looked as though you'd never smile again."

"Well, now, thanks to you," Jill said, "things might start to get better."

"They will," Toni said. "I expect to hear a report shortly that you have become the outstanding freshman—the only freshman to star in the fresh-man play, maintain an A plus average, and be elected Miss Popularity in the same year!"

"You're crazy, you know that?" Jill said.

"Thank heavens." Toni grinned. "I'd die of boredom if I was sane!"

"So would I, Toni," Jill said, laughing as they went up a set of marble steps and in through two big glass doors.

"What's this building?" Toni asked.

"I thought it was appropriate to take you to the gym first," Jill said as she walked toward a set of swinging wooden doors. "If we hurry, maybe we can see the wrestling team practice."

ELEVEN

On Monday morning Jill went to the housing officer. She had spent an uneasy weekend trying to avoid Sheridan and communicating in the shortest possible sentences when she was forced to be with her. Sheridan had spent the weekend making cutting marks about Jill and Toni.

The housing officer was a big woman with lots of chins and a slight British accent. Jill remembered her from the first day at school. She greeted Jill with a nod, so all the chins wobbled.

"Take a seat, Jill. I'm Laura Grant, and I'm in charge of matching people. I gather you don't get on with your roommate," she said, giving Jill a smile.

Jill nodded, wondering what Sheridan had already told Mrs. Grant. "It just doesn't seem to be working out," she said in a small voice. "I'm not the kind of person she wants."

The housing officer laughed. "Don't look so worried about it. It happens all the time. We try to match up people by the way they fill in their forms, but we can make some terrible mistakes. Just because two people play the violin and go to bed late doesn't mean they have the same personalities. I would say a quarter of the freshman class is not happy with our choice, and at least ten pairs are unhappy enough to do something about it. All we have to do is a bit of switching around. Now—do you have someone you'd rather room with?"

Jill shook her head again. "I really haven't had time to make other friends yet."

"Of course you haven't," the housing officer said. "No sense in rushing friendships. The other young lady, Miss Ashley, tells me she has hundreds of friends, so why don't we leave her in the room and let her friends fight out who gets to room with her?" Jill was sure she noticed a twinkle in Mrs. Grant's eyes, as if she might understand the truth about Sheridan Ashley and pity her friends. "And what I suggest we do with you," Mrs. Grant continued, "is put you in the corner room down on the first floor. It's usually a senior room, but it was supposed to be refurbished this summer, and, as usual, nobody got around to it. So it's just sitting there empty until the contractors get to it, which could be forever. Why don't you move in there until you find someone you'd be happy with? Then we can do some switching? How does that sound?"

"Wonderful," Jill said, giving her a beaming smile. "You don't know what a load this is off my mind."

"My dear," Mrs. Grant said, "if you were unhappy, you should have come to me instantly. Nobody is allowed to be miserable at Rosemont. Here, let me give you the key to your room."

She doesn't think it was my fault, Jill thought to herself as she hurried back to McGregor after her classes had ended for the day. She felt as if a huge load had been lifted from her shoulders. When she opened the door to number eleven, she felt even better. It was a corner room with windows on two sides, one looking onto the porch and one out over the lawns. The furniture and walls were shabby but comfortable looking. A braided rug lay on the floor and faded pink drapes hung at the windows.

Sheridan was sitting at her desk when Jill went in to get her belongings. "You'll be pleased to hear I'm moving out," Jill said, taking down the first hangers from the closet."

"Great," Sheridan said flatly, pretending to be busy filing her nails. She didn't offer to help Jill carry anything. When Jill went back upstairs again, she had disappeared.

Jill was exhausted by the time the last load had been moved down, but by bedtime the room looked almost like her own room in Seattle. The ballerina print hung on the wall. Her comforter covered the bed closest to the bathroom. Her clothes were hung neatly in the closet, and her desk had her lamp and her stereo on it.

Jill went to bed feeling relaxed and happy. She lay watching the wisteria vines through her window listening to the sounds of night—a distant car driving past, a burst of laughter from an upstairs room, a group of girls in the lounge singing along to an old record by the Supremes, the creak and settling of the old house. Finally she drifted into sleep.

Jill woke to darkness. The house around her was silent. There were no lights across the campus, except for a streetlight far off, which only let her see the outlines of things in her room. She lay there, wide-awake and alert, wondering what could have woken her. Then she heard the sound again—the sound of somebody outside her window on the front porch.

Probably only cats, she thought, trying to make herself relax. She realized suddenly that her room would be an ideal entry point for burglars. Her heart began to beat quickly. She stared at her window, holding her breath. As she watched, the pane began to slide upward with only a slight scraping sound. Jill was too frightened to move.

I'm in a house full of people. I've only got to scream, and somebody will come, she kept telling herself. But she was too frightened to scream. The window was now fully raised, and a dark figure began to climb in. It seemed to be completely faceless—dark from top to bottom.

Jill could feel her heart thudding in her chest so loudly that she knew the intruder must have heard it, too. She glanced at the door handle, wondering if she could leap up and make it safely to the corridor before the intruder got her. At last she could stand it no longer. As it turned back to close the window, Jill leaped up. The intruder spun around as it heard the noise and screamed. Jill screamed, too. She reached to flip on the light switch. The two of them stood still, blinking in the light, facing each other without moving. When Jill finally stopped shaking, she noticed that the black figure was about her own size—its head covered in a long black shawl. Then it tossed back the shawl, revealing a perfectly ordinarly female, human face beneath it, surrounded by a mane of long, dark hair.

"You scared me to death," said an ordinary girl's voice.

"What are you doing in my room?" Jill managed to ask in a trembling voice.

"I always come in this way," the girl said, looking suspiciously at Jill with huge dark eyes. "This isn't anybody's room. It's empty."

"It's mine now," Jill said. "They moved me in here today."

"I wish somebody had told me," the girl said. "I could have died of heart failure."

"I wish somebody had told me that a strange person was going to be crawling in at one in the morning," Jill said. "I nearly died, too. You try waking up in the middle of the night and seeing a black, faceless figure creeping in through your window!"

The girl started to laugh. Her dark eyes sparkled as she spoke. "I can see what you mean," she said. "I picked up the habit of wearing a shawl when I was in India last summer. It keeps the wind out really well. I must have looked terrifying. But a white figure rising up from a bed didn't look much better!"

Jill started laughing, too. Her knees were feeling weak so she sank back on the edge of the bed. "Why do you come in through my room anyway?" she asked. "Don't you have a key card to the front door like everyone else?"

"I live in two eighteen," the girl said. "But I lost my key card three times the first week. I never did like the idea of pushing a piece of plastic into a slot to get in. It's too space age for me. So I didn't bother to look for it too hard the last time. It's somewhere in my room, but it's just as convenient to go in and out through this window."

"But what were you doing out at this time of night?" Jill asked.

"I need to be on my own sometimes," the girl said. "I can think better at night. I write poems as I walk."

"But all alone at night?" Jill asked. "That's a pretty dumb thing to do. They warned us about not walking around alone after dark."

"This campus is pretty safe, and I can take care of myself," the girl said. "I'm used to being by myself."

"So you walk around writing poetry every night?" Jill said. "Don't you need sleep? Doesn't your roommate worry about you?"

"My roommate snores," the girl said, and a slight smile twitched at her lips. "She'd never notice if I was missing, and I couldn't sleep with that noise anyway."

Jill sensed the unhappiness in her voice. "So you've got roommate problems, too?" she asked. "I had roommate problems, which is why I'm down here."

"What happened?" the girl asked, perching herself on Jill's chair?"

"We just weren't alike," Jill said. "We didn't get along."

"It's tough trying to room with a stranger," the girl agreed. "I'm not used to finding someone else's hair floating in the bathtub. She's a real slob, my roommate!"

Jill nodded. "Mine was the same," she said. "That was one of the reasons we didn't get along."

The girl looked around Jill's room approvingly. "Lucky you with your own room," she said.

"It's only temporary," Jill said. "But I was really enjoying it, until you came in through the window. Look, do you want a cup of hot chocolate? I'm going to get myself some to help me get back to sleep."

"Thanks," the girls said. "It's getting cool outside at night, these days."

"Then take your walks in the evening," Jill said. "You'd be a lot safer that way."

"I can't," the girl said shortly.

"Do you really walk around writing poetry?" Jill asked over her shoulder as she plugged in the coffeepot. "Or do you really go out to meet somebody?"

"Not exactly," the girl said. Jill sensed that she had stumbled onto a topic the girl would rather not have discussed, and they sat in silence until the water boiled. Jill poured the hot water into a mug she had filled with instant cocoa and carried the cup of chocolate to the girl. "Here," she said.

The girl reached out to take it. "Thanks," she murmured.

"Hey, what happened to your hand?" Jill asked. "Did you fall or something?"

The girl parted her hair to examine the long scratch. "A cat scratched me," she said flatly.

"But that's terrible," Jill said. "It might be dangerous. It might have rabies or something."

"It doesn't," the girl said firmly. "It's my cat."

"But pets aren't allowed, are they?" Jill asked.

The girl gazed evenly at Jill. "That's why I can't keep her in the room," she said. "But I couldn't leave her behind, either. She's such a beautiful, sweet cat, and I love her so much. I found her abandoned in the woods behind our house. My mother wanted to take her straight to the animal shelter, of course. She doesn't like animals—they make the place messy. I managed to keep Jelly Bean at home for a couple of weeks until I came to college, but then I had to bring her with me, or she would have been whisked off to the shelter the moment my back was turned."

"But where are you keeping her?" Jill asked.

The girl sighed. "Right now, down in a room found in the basement. I didn't know what else to do. It looks like nobody ever goes there, so she's fairly safe, but it's not the nicest place to be. It will really get cold in winter, and it's boring for a cat to be alone all day. She tried to make a run for the door tonight, and she scratched me when I tried to stop her. I keep looking for somewhere better."

She sat staring down at the steam rising from her hot chocolate. Jill thought about what might happen to people who kept pets in their rooms.

"If I'd had a nicer roommate, maybe I'd have been able to smuggle Jelly Bean into the room," the girl said. "But my roommate is allergic to cats. At least she told me she was." She tossed back her hair and the smile broadened. "I think she's also allergic to me," she said. She took a gulp of the steaming liquid.

"She thinks everything I do is silly, just because I don't happen to like the things she likes."

"I know the feeling," Jill said.

The girl grinned. "My name's Cassandra, by the way, what's yours?"

"Jill."

Cassandra got up. "Well, Jill, I'd better let you get back to sleep," she said. "Thanks for the hot chocolate. I'm sorry I scared you, but I'm really glad we met."

"So am I," Jill said.

"I should go and write my poem down," Cassandra said. "I really do write poetry when I'm walking around, you know. She reached the door and started to open it. Then she turned back. "You won't say anything about my cat, will you?" she pleaded. "I just need a little while until I can figure out what to do with her."

"Of course I won't say anything," Jill said.

Cassandra's face broke into a beaming smile. "I'm glad I came in through your window," she said. "Good night, Jill. Sleep well."

"Good night, Cassandra," Jill said, climbing back into bed.

TWELVE

The next day Cassandra stopped by after dinner to see Jill and stayed talking until after midnight. Jill found her new friend both confusing and fascinating. She had never met anyone like her before. She tried to sort out her thoughts on paper as she wrote to Toni.

"She's so different, Toni, that it's hard to describe her," Jill wrote, sucking at the end of her pen to get her thoughts in order.

She's beautiful in a way, with incredible long black hair, but she doesn't wear any makeup, and her clothes look as if they came from the Salvation Army. But they look good on her. She hates anything phony or plastic.

One thing you notice as soon as you talk to her is that she's crazy about animals. She has a cat she keeps in the basement, but she's looking for a better place for it. I have a horrible feeling she thinks my room might be perfect. I love cats, as you know, but there are no pets allowed on campus.

I didn't realize how much she cared for animals until we went to lunch together today. What a shock that was—we went into the cafeteria together, and I offered her a hamburger. She smiled sweetly and said, "I prefer not to eat the flesh of a murdered animal, thank you, but you go right ahead!" Of course the hamburger didn't taste very good after that, especially as she sat across from me eating alfalfa sprouts and garbanzo beans.

I can't think of anyone in high school who was involved in the way she seems to be. I've only known her a couple of days, and already she's told me about causes I'd never even heard of. She's involved in saving the whales and saving the seals and an effort to prevent logging and stop the draining of a bay marsh. We started talking about foreign travel, and I mentioned that my friend and I had been to Europe this summer. Well, it turned out that she had hitchhiked all through India and had worked there for a month helping a village dig a new well. If she goes on endoctrinating me, I'll probably drop out of school and join the Peace Corps!

If I've made her sound like some spacy health food do-gooder, that's not really it. She just cares for things much more deeply than anyone I ever met before college. But she's so interesting to talk to. We talked for five hours last night and it didn't seem long.

Must stop. My first test in Western civilization coming up tomorrow. Have to sort out my Roman emperors.

Love, Jill.

Jill didn't see Cassandra at all for a couple of days after that. It didn't really surprise her, though. She knew that Cassandra would be the sort of girl who disappeared and reappeared as she wanted to.

Thursday night, around midnight, there was a light tapping at Jill's door. Jill knew instinctively that it was Cassandra on the other side. She put down her reading and walked to the door, prepared to confront Cassandra's latest surprise. Sure enough, when she opened the door, Cassandra was standing there wrapped in her big Indian shawl. Her huge dark eyes looked even larger than usual and very scared.

"Cassandra, what on earth's the matter?" Jill asked, seeing Cassandra's face.

"Can I come in a minute, Jill?" Cassandra asked in a choked voice. "I need someone to talk to."

"Of course, you can come in," Jill said, dragging her inside. "Now tell me what's wrong. You look just terrible."

"I've just had a big fight," Cassandra said. "At least, I've had two big fights."

"Your roommate?" Jill asked.

"That was the second one," Cassandra said, sitting down on the floor with a sigh. "I met the janitor tonight. He saw the light on in the storage room, and he found me feeding Jelly Bean. He's a very weird old man, Jill. He yelled at me a lot. Actually, I think I gave him a shock—I mean, coming in and seeing me crouched on the floor with a black shawl over me and a black cat." She smiled at the memory of it. "Anyway, he said he wanted no strange goings-on in his basement."

"I tried to tell him I was an ordinary girl with an ordinary cat, but he wouldn't listen. He just kept yelling, Jill. It was horrible. I hate people yelling at me. He said that the cat went right out or he'd call the ASPCA."

"So what did you do?" Jill asked.

Cassandra bit her lip. "I tried to persuade my roommate to have the cat in our room, just for tonight. I promised I'd find a place in the morning."

"But she wouldn't agree?"

"Agree?" Cassandra said. "She had hysterics! She threatened to call the R.A. I had to leave right away."

"So where's the cat now?" Jill asked. Cassandra unwrapped her shawl to reveal a fat, black and white cat, curled up in her arms. The cat opened its

127

eyes sleepily, yawned, then curled back into a ball again.

"I don't know what to do now, Jill," Cassandra said. "I don't know where to go. I guess it was dumb of me to think I could smuggle in my cat. My folks are always telling me that I act without thinking. But I had to save her life, didn't I?"

Jill took a deep breath. "You can keep her here if you want to," she said.

Cassandra tossed back her hair. "Look, I know how you feel about rules and things, Jill. You don't have to offer your room."

"We'll try it," Jill said. "I don't want you to lose your cat. I've got a cat at home. I like cats. If it really doesn't work out, then we'll think of something else, but at least you can keep her here for the night."

Cassandra's eyes shone. "You're wonderful, Jill. She won't be any trouble, I promise you. And if anyone makes a fuss, I'll say it was all my fault and you didn't know anything about it."

"You don't have to do that, Cassandra," Jill said. "I'm sure she won't be any trouble. Look how gentle she is."

Cassandra gazed down tenderly as Jill rubbed the big cat under the chin. "She's such a nice cat, Jill. You should have seen her when I found her in the woods. Someone had thrown her out of a car, I'm sure. She was all skin and bones and terrified. But even then she let me pick her up, and she purred. She only wants to lie in the sun all day. She never goes far. And I could come down and see her whenever I wanted to!"

"Look, Cassandra," Jill said hesitantly, "you can move in, too, if you want to."

"I can?" Cassandra asked, beaming. "I'd love to, Jill. I knew the moment I saw you in this room that I wanted to move in, but I didn't dare suggest it because I knew you liked your privacy. But I'm a private person, too. I won't get in your way—honestly. And I have very few possessions, so I won't take up much space! I think I'll go and get my things and move down tonight. You don't know how much I was dreading going back to that room. I was going to sleep on the downstairs sofa."

Jill smiled. She had thought Cassandra was full of confidence and knowledge. But now she was in a scrape and she turned to Jill for help.

By midnight Cassandra was installed as Jill's new roommate. Jill helped her carry down almost no clothes, a floor pillow, an Indian wall hanging, and four crates of books.

"Sorry about these," Cassandra said. "If you want me to keep some of them in the basement, I will, but I can't stand not to be reading something. I even staggered across India with my favorites in my backpack."

"Oh, I like books, too," Jill said, helping to put some on the bookshelves.

Cassandra did not want to contact the housing office about her move, but Jill finally insisted that she do it the next day.

As they arranged the room in the morning, Jill remembered she was to meet with Dr. Hollomon to discuss her first report. She told Cassandra of her dread. Other students, who had already received their grades, were displaying papers full of red comments, cross-outs, and exclamation marks.

"Why should you be afraid of any teacher?" Cassandra asked in amazement. "After all, he is supposed to teach you. That's his job. He wouldn't even be here if there weren't any students. You tell him that if he's rude."

Jill couldn't see herself saying that to any professor, especially not to one like Dr. Holloman, who looked as if he ate freshmen for breakfast. But it did make her feel better to recall Cassandra's comments as she knocked timidly on the professor's door.

"Come in, Miss Gardner," Dr. Hollomon commanded. He pointed silently to a seat. Before him was Jill's paper, covered in red ink.

At least it's not in the wastebasket, Jill thought as he handed it to her. *I suppose I should be grateful for that*. She took it and started to read the comments: "Too obvious!" "Cliché!" "Juvenile comment!" "You

mentioned this before: we don't need it twice!"
"*Wrong!*"

Jill swallowed hard and put down the paper.

"Any comments?" Dr. Holloman asked, eyeing her over his rimless glasses.

Jill opened her mouth and tried to force out the words. "I thought I made some valid points, but you seem to have disagreed with everything," she said. "Surely you can't say I'm wrong all the time because neither of us knows for certain what Shakespeare really intended."

Dr. Holloman looked at her hard. Jill felt her knees quaking under the table.

Then he smiled. "We only disagree on minor points, Miss Gardner," he said. "Actually I thought this was pretty sound. Most students wouldn't have had the nerve to choose Shakespeare for a first topic. But I do think you have a feeling for Shakespeare and enough knowledge to back up your statements. This was an interesting paper, Miss Gardner. I look forward to your next one."

Jill looked at the sea of red ink and mumbled her thanks. As she got up to go, Dr. Holloman looked up suddenly. "By the way, Miss Gardner, the copy shop over at the student press needs some extra help," he said. "I thought you might be someone who wants to supplement her income."

"Oh," Jill stammered. "That would be great— thank you."

"Then I'll give them your name," he said. "Go down and see them this afternoon. I don't want any of my better students worrying about money. It distracts them from their work." And the ghost of a smile flickered over his lips.

Jill emerged from the office in a daze. *This,* she thought, *is what college should be like. I just had an intellectual conversation with my toughest professor. Now I'm going to get a job at the student press* . Toni had been right. Everything was changing for the better.

THIRTEEN

"So how was your first evening of slave labor?" Cassandra asked Jill the next Monday as Jill walked into the room.

"Not bad at all," Jill said, taking off her jacket and hanging it on the back of the door. "In fact, it was a piece of cake. There's a manager called Mr. Allen who runs the place and just a couple of other students who work there. Mr. Allen thinks all students are idiots. You should have seen him explaining how to write up an order and how to stack paper."

Cassandra laughed. "That doesn't sound too hard," she said.

"I think it's going to be fine," Jill agreed. "I get to earn money and to meet more people."

Jill found herself alone in the shop with Mr. Allen on Wednesday, her third evening of work. As she glanced out of the window, she noticed couples walking by hand in hand. She had had hardly any time to miss Craig the first weeks of school, but now she did. Most of the spring and summer, she had thought she would be going to college parties with him, strolling with him around the campus, studying next to him in the library, whispering good night to him as they parted on the steps of her dormitory. Now, every time she talked to him on the phone, she was very conscious of his noisy house in the background and her own position in the hallway. Neither one of them felt free to say, "I love you" when half a college was walking past.

Jill sighed again and returned to stacking papers. Mr. Allen came up behind her.

"Did Bob go already?"

"Yes," Jill said.

"Another party, I suppose," Mr. Allen said with a snort. "These kids. They're good workers until they start making friends, then suddenly it's party time! No more workers. Same every year. I don't know why I don't just open a nice, peaceful print shop in town instead of putting up with you students. Now I've got the college newspaper to put to bed. Did they deliver that copy yet?"

Jill looked around. "Nobody delivered anything while I was here," she said.

"Stupid kids," Mr. Allen muttered. "How can I print their newspaper for them if I don't have a last page? Would you run over to the newspaper office and tell them that I need that last page right now if they want a paper this week!"

"Where's the office?" Jill asked.

"Fine arts building in the basement. Go down the steps at the back," Mr. Allen said.

Just as Jill was opening the door marked "The Voice," someone yelled, "Oh, heck!" and a white missile whizzed past her head and struck the wall. She gasped in fright and looked up to see a long-haired boy in a torn Rosemont sweat shirt sitting at a desk, staring up at her.

"I'm sorry about that," he said with an embarrassed smile. "Don't think I was aiming at you. I wasn't expecting anyone to walk in. I've been hurling wads of paper at the wall all evening."

Jill returned his smile. "It's OK," she said. "I think my heart's started beating again."

"Did you want something?" he asked. "Dumb question. I mean, nobody would walk down this hall by mistake at nine P.M., would they?"

"Mr. Allen over at the print shop sent me," Jill said, her eyes wandering over the clutter of the room. Papers on every surface, including the floor, competed with half-eaten slices of pizza and empty soda cans for prominence. "He asked me to tell you that he needs the last page of the paper right now."

"I know he does," the boy growled. "That's been my problem. I've been expecting an article for the back page, but when the guy finally turned it in, it was three pages of garbage. There's no way I can use it. I mean, how can I squeeze three badly written pages on the history of Rosemont's tennis team into four column inches? So I've been sitting here, all alone, staring at four empty column inches on my paste-up, and my brain is totally empty."

Jill walked over to look at the paste-up board resting on piles of scribbled papers. "Couldn't you put in an advertisement or something?" she asked.

The boy pushed his hair back from his forehead. "Trying to get ads for this paper is like squeezing blood out of a stone. The only people who'll advertise are pizza parlors, and their limit is one ad per issue."

"We used to have a little humor column on the back page of my paper at high school," Jill suggested. "You know, making fun of one of the teachers or something that happened around school. Have you considered doing something like that?"

"I'll try anything," the boy said. "Cooking recipes, love letters, I don't care what it is as long as it fills up four column inches." He looked up suddenly at Jill. "Did you write for your paper back at school?"

"Yes," Jill said.

He reached out and handed her a blank piece of paper. "You write me a humor column then," he said.

"You're joking, aren't you?" Jill asked, embarrassed.

The boy looked at her. "No, I'm not. I need copy right now, and it's just you and me and the typewriter here, and I've been trying for the past two hours. Write me anything. Anything would be better than four blank inches. Just give me a freshman's impressions, you are a freshman, aren't you, or something—anything—in a hurry."

"Well, OK," Jill said, sitting down hesitantly on the edge of a desk. "I'll try if you're desperate."

"Believe me, I'm desperate. Do this, and I'll be your slave for life. I'm Russel, by the way. What's your name?"

"I'm Jill," Jill said. "Do you have a pencil? I can only write creative stuff in pencil."

He handed her one with an amused look, and Jill started scribbling while Russel paced behind her. After a while she handed the paper back to him. "I don't know if this is at all what you want," she said. "I used to write for my paper back in high school, but it's probably juvenile stuff compared to your articles."

Russel began reading: "Leading ornithologists have reported numerous sightings of the rare freshman bird on the Rosemont campus.

"This bird is distinguished by its new plumage. It's usually green and wet behind the ears.

"It can be spotted scurrying from roost to roost, glancing fearfully around to make sure it is going to the right place.

"Its food preferences are strange. It actually goes regularly to the cafeteria to feed and must have unusually strong digestive powers.

"Its call is a distinctive, 'Am I in the right place?'"

Russel burst out laughing and flung down the paper. "That's magnificent, Jill. It's terrific. Just what the back page needs! Listen, how would you like to write me a regular column. I'll give you more than four inches if you write like that!"

"I'd really like to write for the paper, Russel," Jill said, feeling her cheeks flush with pleasure. She stood by Russel while he typed up her piece, feeling a renewed glow of pride as he added, "By Jill Gardner, freshman correspondent."

FOURTEEN

Dear Jill,

Don't faint, but I'm actually writing you a letter. My mom says we have to cut down on phone bills, so I'm trying out a new form of communication. Well, that's about long enough for my first letter. My hand is tired. Bye, Jill.

Ha, ha. Just kidding! I was dying to phone you last night. My mom was out, and Dad was watching TV in the den. I kept looking at the phone all evening, but I was a good daughter and didn't use it.

But I have to tell you the good news—I have a job! Furthermore, I've had the job three days, and I haven't been fired yet. Is this a record? It must be, especially when you hear what the job is: I'm a waitress for a fancy catering company! Imagine me, serving weddings and cocktail parties. I bet you can't imagine it. I couldn't, either. But I met this super-cute boy when I was at the college getting my catalog, and he told me how much money he makes as a waiter. Naturally I thought it might be a good idea to see more of him, so I went down for an interview. I told him I'd had tons of experience—on roller skates, too. (I didn't mention the collision and the french fries sailing through the air!) Even more amazing is that I've already worked two parties without a disaster. The only minor accident was when a salmon mousse in the shape of a fish slid off a tray as I picked it up in the kitchen. I tried to scrape it up and mold it back into a fishy shape, but it looked really revolting, so I just scooped up the mess and washed it down the sink. Nobody seemed to notice that they didn't get any salmon. One man even gave me a ten-dollar tip at the end of the evening!

So life seems to be starting up again. I'm going to register this week. I really can't decide what classes to take. A lot of them look like fun, but I suppose I should do required courses instead. Hope life is going well with you. I met a gorgeous rich guy at my party last night—unfortunately it was a wedding, and he was the groom! The next function might be a bachelor party. I've always wanted to come out of a cake.

Love, Toni.

P.S. This is the longest thing I have ever

written in my life, including my report on the Civil War!"

Dear Toni,

I got your letter just as I was about to write to you. Isn't that funny? It must be telepathy, I guess. I'm glad things are starting to go well for you—also amazed that you are a waitress. That is not exactly the career choice I would have made for you, having seen what you can do with a jar of bubble bath!

Life goes along very smoothly with Cassandra. She's such a private person that I hardly even know she's around, and yet she's wise enough that I can talk to her if I need advice.

I've also been busy getting myself a job—or rather two jobs. My English teacher got me an evening job at the campus printing shop—not printing anything, just taking money and filing things, so it's not hard work. I'm also writing for the college news-paper, which I got into entirely by accident. I've been signed up to write a freshman column for the back page. The second one comes out tomorrow, Thursday. I did a piece on college food. You can't go far wrong criticizing that! I tried to make it funny, pretending the greatest detectives in the world had been called in to analyze what's in college food. I had Hercule Poirot and Sherlock Holmes trying to find clues to the unidentified floating substances in the pot pies and Sam Spade waiting in the shadows all night to find out what they put in pancakes to make them bounce.

Do you think I'll make a name for myself as the Lois Lane of Rosemont? I haven't noticed too many Supermen around yet. Talk to you soon. I'm planning a weekend home before long. I need some of my mother's cooking.

Love, Jill.

The weekly edition of the Rosemont *Voice* appeared around campus by midmorning that Thursday. Students were passing around copies during Jill's English class and giggling at her article. Dr. Hollomon interrupted his lecture to peer at the class over his spectacles.

"May I ask what you are reading that is so funny?" he demanded. "Certainly it isn't *Hamlet*, because none of you appear to understand that."

"It's an article in the student newspaper, Dr. Hollomon," one girl in the front row said. "I'm sorry. It was very funny."

"I didn't realize we had such good writers on our student newspaper," Dr. Hollomon said dryly. "Anyone who can take your attention away from Shakespeare must be really outstanding."

Jill found herself blushing scarlet in the back row, but no more was said. A few students glanced around and grinned at her. At the end of class several hung around to walk with her to the cafeteria.

"How did that feel, to be compared to Shakespeare?" a tall boy asked.

"He was only making fun," Jill said. "I hope he doesn't find out I wrote the article."

"I thought it was good," the boy said. "You live in McGregor, don't you? I thought I'd seen you in the hall. I'm Robert, and he's Jason, and we're on the third floor. Now that I know you're a writer, I'll be down for help with my essays."

They reached the cafeteria together.

"We're going to stick with you from now on," Jason said. "Matter of survival. We'll watch what you eat and avoid everything else." They went through the line as a laughing, noisy group and sat at a table together. Other students passed them with trays, and many of them were talking about the article.

"Looks like you've got a hit on your hands," Robert said. "Everyone is talking about it."

"I'd no idea it would make this much of an impression," Jill said, feeling her cheeks turn pink as strangers pointed her out across the cafeteria. "I thought complaining about college food was an old, old topic."

"But maybe nobody's ever put it in print," a girl named Becky said.

Robert grinned. "It'll be interesting to find out what happens to you," he said. "I won't be surprised if the secret police come around in the night and you're never seen again."

Jason nodded seriously. "Or she'll come back years later after they've broken and brainwashed her, and she'll stand on the cafeteria steps and admit she was wrong. Then she'll eat a whole slice of pizza to prove it."

"Oh, be quiet, you guys are making me nervous," Jill said. "There's freedom of speech on a college campus, isn't there?"

"You'll find out soon enough," Robert said. "Is it really true that the pancake bounced?"

"I saw it," Jill said. "It dropped onto its edge and bounced before it started rolling."

"I believe it," a large redheaded boy passing the table said. "I'd believe anything about this cafeteria."

"The way you eat, Flame, you don't care what the food tastes like! It goes past your tastebuds too

144

quick for them to notice," the boy next to him said. The others all laughed.

"Yeah, he even eats the beet Jell-O!" another boy added, pointing at the round, red mass sitting in a sundae dish on his tray.

The redhead looked surprised. "Is that beet? Nobody ever told me that. I hate beets!"

The others all burst out laughing.

"It's not funny, you guys," the redhead said. "What sort of friends are you if you don't stop someone from eating beets. Come to think of it, I always thought this stuff was disgusting." He put down his tray on Jill's table and picked up the sundae dish. "I wonder if beet Jell-O bounces as well as pancakes," he suggested. He turned it upside down experimentally. The beet Jell-O didn't even move. The boys laughed even louder. "There it is, Flame—it's stuck forever," one boy yelled.

"You're right," Flame admitted. "I bet they use Super Glue." He gave the glass a mighty shake. The beet Jell-O flew out and landed on the crowd at the next table, splattering a white T-shirt with an impressive beet-colored stain. The girls at the table leaped up. The boy with the beet-splattered T-shirt leaped up, too.

"I suppose you think that's real funny, Flame," he growled.

"Hey, man, I'm sorry. It was an accident," Flame said, grinning. "We were doing an experiment with beet Jell-O—"

"Oh, really," the boy growled. "How interesting. Let's see if the chocolate pudding flies as well as the beet Jell-O!" Before anyone could stop him, he had picked up his dish and thrown the sticky brown mess at Flame. It hit him square in the face and oozed dark brown down his shirtfront.

"Now you've really asked for it," the boys standing with Flame yelled. "Try some mashed potato."

A girl screamed as the white blob sailed through the air, splattering everyone in its path. Someone yelled, "Food fight!" and suddenly the whole cafeteria was full of flying food. All the participants yelled and screamed half in delight as they struck their targets, half in horror as lasagna or broccoli hit them in the faces.

"These biscuits are better than baseballs," someone was shouting behind Jill. "Watch me throw a curve ball!"

"Cut it out, you guys," a girl pleaded before she was hit in the face with a plate of ice cream. Water and milk glasses were knocked over. The floor was a slippery mess of fallen food. Students who tried to make their way to the exits and safety sat down instead on piles of macaroni salad. Others fell over them. Within minutes the room looked like the scene of a violent massacre, with red and yellow goo dripping from walls, and chairs and bodies lying everywhere.

At that moment the campus police arrived on the scene. "Cool it right now, everybody," blasted a voice through a bullhorn. "Or we turn the hoses on you."

"Everybody quiet or we make some arrests," the voice went on.

One by one the students lowered their weapons and stood examining the wreckage. "What has been going on here?" demanded another voice, and the dean of students stepped past the police and into the cafeteria.

"You should be ashamed of yourselves," the dean said, stepping delicately over the piles of food on the floor. "Acting like savages. Is this what I can expect of Rosemont students? If it is, I don't know why I bother. I'll go and work in the state prison next year—they behave better there."

"Their food's better, too," someone growled.

"What was that?" asked the dean.

"He said the food's better in state prison," a student near the front said. "And he's right. That's how this whole thing started, with the article on how bad our food is."

The dean frowned. "So, you are trying to tell me that this is a form of protest then?" he asked.

"Yes," someone ventured. "That's right—it was a protest. The food here is inedible."

"Protest is healthy," he said, "but only when handled in a mature way. This was a childish form of protest. Destroying and vandalizing achieve nothing. You have student council and student media if you wish to express opinions."

Jill had been trapped in her place, horrified but unable to move throughout the whole fight. Now she was aware of faces turned in her direction.

"If you wish to pursue this matter further," the dean said, "have it brought up through your elected representatives. In the meantime I suggest you go to the kitchen, get every mop and bucket you can find, and clean up this mess!"

FIFTEEN

Jill spent a very tense afternoon cleaning up the cafeteria, even though she hadn't thrown any food. Several students had approached her to tell her that she had been very brave to write her article. Jill didn't feel brave at all. She had gone through high school without ever having had to appear before the principal. She would have gone through all of elementary school with a spotless record, too, if she hadn't been involved in a fight the first day Toni had arrived. As she sponged the last of the spaghetti from her sweat shirt, she was sick with fright. She could almost hear the dean's voice, "We do not welcome troublemakers at this campus, Miss Gardner. When we offered you a place here, we thought you would be grateful to us and work hard. But it seems you only came to Rosemont to make trouble."

Sheridan Ashley passed Jill as she walked back to the dorm, her hair wet and tangled and her hands stinging from detergent. Sheridan had not spoken to Jill since the day Jill moved. "I hear you're in trouble again!" she said now. "You sure do like to stir things up!" She walked off with a grin on her face.

By dinner time it seemed that almost everyone on campus knew Jill. Much to her horror, some people asked, "Were you the one who started that fight?"

"You wanted to meet more people," Cassandra said. "Now you've got your wish."

"I know, it's terrible," Jill said. "I can't show my face in the cafeteria again in case they think I'm setting up another riot. Imagine being expelled for causing a riot. I've been biting my nails all afternoon and waiting to be called to the dean's office."

Cassandra took hold of her shoulders. "Look, Jill, you have nothing to be ashamed of. You made good points in your article. Everyone agreed with everything you said. Maybe now the college will improve the food!" As they rounded the corner to go to the cafeteria, she gripped Jill's arm. "What's that?" she asked.

A group of students were walking up and down outside the cafeteria, carrying signs. "BOYCOTT COLLEGE FOOD," one sign said. "DON'T EAT HERE TILL GARBAGE DISAPPEARS." "DEAN PLEASE NOTE—THIS IS AN ORDERLY PROTEST. NOW GO IMPROVE THE FOOD." "'PANCAKES SHOULD NOT BOUNCE'—JULIA CHILD."

Some students were arriving at the cafeteria, reading the signs, and walking away again. Others hung around in interested groups.

"Looks like you really did start something," Cassandra commented.

"Oh, no," Jill gasped. "Look over there at that sign."

"You wanted to be well known on campus," Cassandra said. "You can't be more well known than that." A girl was walking toward them carrying a sign that read, "JILL GARDNER TELLS IT LIKE IT IS."

At that moment Russel and two other boys came running across the grass, waving their arms and yelling.

"We've just come from the dean's office," one of them panted. "He's agreed to listen to our complaints."

"He's going to have someone monitor the food for the rest of this semester, and he's putting a complaint book in the cafeteria so we can let him know what food is really bad."

"You did it, Jill," Russel shouted to her. "Victory party over in my room in Phillips tonight! Eight o'clock—and we'll order in pizza! Real pizza that doesn't break teeth!"

"You will come, won't you?" a girl holding a sign asked Jill. "You'll be guest of honor."

"Sure," Jill mumbled, embarrassed by all the attention. "Thanks, I'd like to."

It was only after she had walked away that she remembered her job.

"Can I leave early tonight?" she ventured to Mr. Allen. "There's a big party over in Phillips. I've been specially invited, and I told them I'd go, so could you do without me after seven-thirty?"

"There you are," Mr. Allen boomed. "What did I tell you? Every year it's the same. You get a good freshman for a couple of weeks at the most, and suddenly it's parties, parties, parties."

"Oh, I won't be like that, Mr. Allen, I promise you," Jill pleaded. "It's just that this is a special party, and I did work until ten for Bob the other night."

"That's what they always say," Mr. Allen said, sighing. "They always tell me it's 'Just this once, Mr. Allen,' but I know the beginning of the end when I see it."

"Oh." Jill turned away disappointed. "I guess I can't go then."

"Come back here," Mr. Allen yelled after her. "Just because I know the beginning of the end doesn't mean I won't let you off early. I'm resigned to the beginning of the end by now."

"Oh, Mr. Allen, thank you," Jill said, beaming. "I'll work extra hard and try to get everything done before I leave."

He smiled at her enthusiasm. "You're a good worker anyway," he said. "You do more than your share."

By eight o'clock Jill was almost ready for the party. She had decided on her favorite gray cotton jump suit and had caught her long reddish brown hair back in two combs.

"I wish you'd come," Jill said to Cassandra as she dressed. "I won't know a soul there."

"I have an enormous physics test tomorrow," Cassandra said, picking up her book once more.

"Then I guess I'll have to go alone," Jill said. "But I won't stay long. It's going to be mostly a senior party, anyway, so I'll show up for a while, then leave."

"Go enjoy yourself," Cassandra said.

As Jill turned into Phillips Hall, a huge blast of sound greeted her through the open front door. The downstairs lounge was packed with students. Music from a stereo was fighting with the shouts and laughter. As she stood hesitantly in the doorway, hands grabbed her. "Here she is! Jill's here," someone yelled, and Russel appeared through the crowd.

"Great!" He beamed. "We were waiting for you. Come and meet everybody. Hey, everyone, this is

the star writer who has saved you all from th
torment of cafeteria food!"

Suddenly a crowd collected around Jill. Peop
she didn't recognize wanted to know where she ha
come from and what she felt about Rosemont. Sh
heard herself as if from a distance, describing he
high school newspaper as if it were a real
important contribution to journalism, instead
just a mimeographed sheet which she folded an
stapled herself.

I'm being a phony, she thought. *The kind of pers*
Cassandra would really dislike. She made an excuse
move toward the drink table and poured herself
tall glass of soda. Someone tried to take it from he
hand. "Not soda," Russel said. "Tonight we a
celebrating. Have some champagne."

"I really don't drink," Jill mumbled.

"Correction, you didn't drink," the boy stand
ing with Russel said, laughing. "Everybody
Rosemont drinks. If they find out you don't drin
they expel you instantly."

"Besides," Russel said seriously. "This is def
nitely a special occasion. Go on, try some."

Jill took a sip. The fizzy bubbles tingled on he
tongue.

"So how do you like it?" Russel's frien
demanded.

"It's a lot better than beer," Jill admitted. Th
boy laughed as if she had said something ver

funny. "You see, you do belong at Rosemont. You have expensive tastes," he said. "I'm Hank. I'm also a writer, but somewhat more serious than newspapers."

"Oh, what do you write?" Jill asked.

"Plays mainly. I wrote a play for the playwrights festival last year."

"And it was terrible," a voice cut in. "Two men on a railway station waiting for a train for three whole acts. I thought I had better come and rescue you before this man bores you to death."

Jill looked up to find herself staring into Kyle's startlingly blue eyes.

"Get out of here, Robertson. I saw her first," Hank said.

Kyle looked down at Jill, and she noticed how his eyes crinkled attractively at the sides when he smiled. "Sorry," he said, "but Jill and I are old friends. As a matter of fact, we met on the very first freshman orientation day, didn't we, Jill?"

The other boy groaned. "Trust Robertson not to waste any time," he said. "Now we know why you always volunteer to come back early—you like to get your pick of freshman girls."

"Of course," Kyle said. "I'm not stupid, you know, and I have excellent taste." He slipped his arm around Jill's shoulders as he was talking. "I saw she was the only freshman worth watching this year."

Hank burst out laughing. "What about Jenny what's-her-name?" he spluttered.

Kyle continued smiling. "Definitely not worth watching. Come on, Jill, you and I are going to get at that pizza before those pigs finish it."

He whisked Jill through the crowd, and she didn't protest. She didn't know if she wanted to. "That food fight was terrific," Kyle said, handing Jill a big slice of pizza dripping with cheese. "I haven't had so much fun all year. What are you going to think up next for my enjoyment?" His blue eyes looked down at her with amusement.

"Oh, look, I never intended—" Jill stammered, very conscious of the effect he was having on her and feeling uneasy about it.

"Kyle, are you hogging the guest of honor as usual?" Russel demanded, pushing between them. "You can't have her all to yourself tonight. It's my party. Come and get some more champagne, Jill." He took her arm very firmly.

Jill looked back at Kyle. "You want to leave these creeps and go for a drive?" Kyle asked, smiling at her. "My car's right outside."

"No, she is not going anywhere," Russel said. "And I certainly wouldn't trust the poor girl with you. She's only a freshman, remember. She's not used to the big, wide world yet."

"Oh, she's very mature for her age, I can tell. Aren't you, Jill?" he asked. "Don't you want to come for a drive with me?"

Jill looked from Kyle to the other students around them. It seemed like an amazing step to have people fighting over her suddenly.

"Will you quit bugging her?" Russel said. "I'm her editor, and I forbid her to go out tonight."

Kyle's smile did not falter. "How about the day after tomorrow then, Jill?" he asked. "I'm going to this great party. Do you want to come with me? You'd have a wonderful time."

Jill was conscious of a lot of people looking at her. She thought of Russel's comment that she was not ready for the big, wide world. If she could write articles that received attention all over campus, certainly she could handle herself at a party. She smiled at Kyle. "Sure," she said. "Why not?"

SIXTEEN

Jill woke the next morning to somebody shaking her.

"Wake up, Jill, you're wanted on the phone!" Cassandra's face swam into focus.

"What time is it?" Jill asked, sitting up with her heart pounding.

"Seven-thirty," Cassandra said calmly.

"Oh," Jill said. "For a minute I thought I'd slept through my first class. Who would be calling me at seven-thirty?"

"Don't ask me," Cassandra said, handing Jill her robe. "I just heard your name being yelled, that's all. It woke me up, but not you. You must have had a big time last night."

"I didn't get back until after midnight," Jill admitted, slipping on her robe and tying it around her.

Cassandra gave a knowing smile. "And you told me you'd be back early because you wouldn't know anybody," she said. "You must have met someone who persuaded you to stay on."

"I'll tell you later," Jill said and ran down the hall to the phone.

"Wake up, sleepyhead!" Toni's voice boomed down the phone.

"Toni, I can't believe it!" Jill shouted. "You have ESP. I have so much to tell you." She quickly recounted the previous day's activities.

"So you must be some sort of folk hero now, I guess," Toni suggested.

"Well, I've met a lot of people because of it—upperclassmen want to talk to me now, when most of the time they step over freshmen as if they're worms."

"Like that guy on the motorbike?" Toni asked.

"Funny you should mention him," Jill said hesitantly. "Because we had a great time together last night, and he's invited me to a party tomorrow. A really fancy party for his rich friend's birthday."

"You're not going, are you?" Toni asked, horrified.

"Well," Jill said, "don't you think I should?"

"But what about Craig?"

"Toni Redmond, you're always the one who tells me I'm crazy to stick to one boy. Now I'm following your advice, and you don't like it."

"Look, Jill," Toni began. "You know I'm not crazy about you and Craig turning into an old married couple, but I really don't think you should go to this party."

"Why not?" Jill demanded. "Toni—I'm just going to a party with a guy, that's all. I'm not betraying Craig. He goes to parties without me. This will be a totally new experience for me. It will be a party just like the ones you serve at. This is a twenty-first birthday party for a friend of Kyle's over in Portland. I've never been to a party like that. Kyle says this family always throws fantastic parties. They're going to have an orchestra and circus acts and a complete outside dance floor. Imagine me, drifting around under the stars in a long dress."

"In somebody's arms who isn't Craig," Toni warned.

"Toni! No one could compare with Craig as far as I'm concerned. Besides, I just met the guy, really, but he is a lot of fun."

"The truth is, Jill, I don't think he's your type of person," Toni said.

"How would you know?"

"I saw the way he behaved. He's a spoiled brat, and he thinks he's wonderful."

"He's not as bad as that, Toni. He was a lot of fun last night, and I don't plan to get involved with him."

"Ha!" Toni said emphatically. "I know you too well, Jill Gardner, and your trouble is that you do get involved. Look at Carlo. Anyone else would have had a pleasant European vacation romance, but, no, you have to fall madly in love, and I had to spend days swimming my way through gallons of tears and mending a broken heart. I don't want either of us to go through that again."

"I don't intend to go through that again," Jill said. "I'm a big girl now, Toni. I'm a college student. I'm growing up. You've got to trust me to make my own friends and my own decisions."

"Only when I think you know best," Toni said. "And this time you don't. Guys like Kyle, who don't care who they run down with their motorbikes, are all spoiled rotten and selfish. Every party I work at I have to fight my way out of the kitchen where I'm trapped by some big oaf in a tux. And the rest of the time these guys order you around as if you're a slave, or they don't even notice you exist. One fat guy who'd been trying to grab me behind the refrigerator knocked over a glass ten minutes later and said to his friend, 'Oh, don't bother about that. The girl will clean it up,' just as if I were Cinderella. I'd much rather date Brian any day."

"Brian?"

"He's the guy I told you about—the one who's the waiter with me and going to community college, too. He's sweet. Like a teddy bear." She paused. "He's a bit boring, to tell you the truth, but he's comforting for now—very solid and dependable."

Jill laughed. "It's funny how things switch around, isn't it?" she asked. "Did you ever think that you'd be going with the solid dependable guy and I'd have the wild, crazy one?"

"Never," Toni said. "And I only hope you won't find you're making a big mistake."

"You'd be surprised," Jill said. "I'm changing. I had a good time at that party last night, and you know how I normally am at parties. I really liked being the center of attention, Toni. It felt good to have all those people crowding around me. So give me a chance to come out of my cocoon and turn into a butterfly, will you? Don't try to spoil things for me."

"I've never wanted to do that," Toni said. "It's just that I've been through enough emotion for a while. I don't think I could stand it if you got yourself into a crisis. Oh, no! Listen, take care of yourself. I've got to go."

"I will, Toni," Jill said. "And don't worry."

I've spent all my life being good old sensible Jill, Jill thought as she hung up the phone. *It's about time I had some fun!* Other students didn't worry all the time about good grades. They went to parties and still managed to get through all their classes. *From now on,* Jill thought, *the world will see the new, improved Jill Gardner! You wait until you see me next time, Toni Redmond. You'll hardly recognize me.*

SEVENTEEN

By seven o'clock Saturday evening, Jill was ready, waiting for Kyle.

"I won't ask you how I look," Jill said to Cassandra. "Because you'll only tell me you've never been to a party like this, so you've got no idea."

Cassandra looked up as Jill came out of the bathroom. "I've had to suffer through lots of parties like that. My mother loves giving them. You'll do just fine."

"It was my prom dress," Jill said. "I thought it looked so sophisticated then. Now I'm not so sure."

"It looks very nice," Cassandra said. "That color really highlights your chestnut hair. Besides, who cares who likes the dress, as long as you do?"

"I shouldn't care, but I do," Jill said. "I want people to think I look nice. I'm not like you, Cassie."

"I know that," Cassandra said. "I would hate it. I'm glad it's you who's going and not me!"

"I can hardly wait," Jill said. "I wish Kyle would get here. He said seven o'clock and it's already ten after."

By seven-thirty Kyle still hadn't arrived. Cassandra sat curled up in her chair like a cat, calmly reading while Jill paced up and down. Jill glanced in the mirror and realized that she had chewed off all her lipstick. She went through to the bathroom to put more on. Kyle chose that moment to arrive.

"Aren't you ready yet?" he called as he came in. "Come on, we've got a long drive, you know."

"Her makeup faded while she waited for you," Cassandra said dryly from her chair.

"Am I late?" he asked, looking at his watch. "Oh, well, I guess I am. Are you ready, Jill?"

Jill appeared and a smile spread over Kyle's face. "You look just right," he said. "Let's get going."

Jill thought Kyle looked just right, as well, in a black tuxedo and pleated white shirt. He took her hand and led her down the hall.

"Hey, you look nice," one of the girls commented as they walked past. "Where's the party? Are we missing something?"

"It's in Portland, and you are not invited, Heather Hodgson," Kyle yelled as he dragged Jill down the steps. "We're already late," he said to Jill. "Paul's mother hates it when guests don't arrive on time."

He led Jill toward a black Corvette. The moment they climbed in, he gunned the engine and the car shot forward with great force.

"Aren't you worried about getting a ticket?" Jill asked hesitantly as they roared toward the highway. "We're going awfully fast."

"It's OK," Kyle said. "I've only got one on my record right now. I can get another two before they suspend my license, and my dad is a lawyer, so he can usually get me out of things." He swung the car around a corner so violently that the tires screeched in protest. He roared down the block, narrowly missing a pedestrian.

"You get an extra ten points for old ladies," he said, grinning across at Jill. Then he noticed her face. "Hey, relax. I'm a great driver. I can handle this thing perfectly. And I also know which stretch of road the cops work. You've got nothing to worry about."

He glanced over at Jill, who was still gripping the door handle, and laughed. "I should have opened a bottle of champagne for us before we left," he said. "That's what relaxed you last night, wasn't it? You were floating!"

Was it true, Jill wondered. Had she only had such a good time because of the champagne? She tried to think about the evening's events, but her concentration was devoted to stopping herself from being flung around the car every time they went round a corner.

She was relieved when the car finally came to a halt outside a large house on a tree-lined street.

Scores of expensive cars were already parked all around, but Kyle pulled up to the front door and helped Jill out while the engine still ran.

"Find someone to park this," he said to a maid as he led Jill into the house. They had almost reached the end of a long hallway decorated with big vases of flowers and marble statues when a beautiful, tall woman emerged from a doorway at the back. Her hair was piled into a mass of curls, every one perfectly in place. Her face was expertly made up, and her plain white silk dress was adorned only by a large emerald at her neck. She smiled thinly as she saw Kyle and Jill.

"Kyle, how lovely. Paul was so worried that you weren't going to make it. And who is this charming young lady? She extended a white-gloved hand to shake Jill's.

"Gardner," she repeated when Kyle introduced them. "Then you can't be an Oregonian. I don't know any Gardners, except the sort that dig up flowers instead of weeds," she added with a musical little laugh.

Jill explained that she was from Seattle, and immediately the woman described a yacht race she had once seen in that city. "Did you catch that one?" she asked Jill.

"Oh, no," Jill admitted, feeling slightly dishonest not confessing that she had never seen any yacht race.

"Oh," the woman said as if she had guessed Jill's secret. "Well, everyone else is outside. Do come out and meet everybody."

The lawn was decorated like something from a movie. Lanterns hung from all the trees. In the middle gleamed a huge dance floor, while an orchestra sat playing beside the pool. Hundreds of young people, all in formal dress, stood talking while waiters and waitresses moved among them with trays of food and drink. One or two couples danced halfheartedly.

A thin, sandy-haired young man detached himself from the rest and ran toward Kyle. "Glad you could make it, big fellow," he said, slapping Kyle on the back. "We thought you'd been imprisoned in that dump or something. And you've brought someone I've never met before. Is she my birthday present?"

"Hand's off, Paul," Kyle said. "It may be your birthday, but I don't share my dates. Anyway, my mother already sent you a gift from the whole family."

"Those measly gold cuff links don't count as a gift," Paul said, laughing. "Anyway, I get the first dance with her, whoever she is. Birthday boy's treat. Come on, whoever you are."

"I'm Jill," she said, laughing nervously as he led her across to the dance floor.

"And I'm Paul," he said, wrapping his arms around her as they started to move to the slow beat. "I haven't seen you at any of our things before. Are you new to the area?"

"I'm a freshman at Rosemont," Jill said.

Paul's face fell. "Oh, no," he said. "Am I dancing with a brain?"

"Oh, I'm very ordinary," Jill said. "I just squeezed into Rosemont."

Paul smiled. "Daddy pulled some strings?" He laughed. "That's how Kyle got in, too. He didn't have the grades, but his dad donated so much to the library that they suddenly found a place for him."

And almost kept people like me out, Jill thought.

The dance ended to polite clapping, and Paul started to lead her back to Kyle, who was now surrounded by a group of girls.

"Let me get you some champagne before I hand you over again," Paul said, squeezing her arm. "I need some, too, before I tackle the next dance. My mother says that I have to dance with every girl at least once. Aren't parties like this a bore? I wanted to take a few people to the mountains for my birthday, but I couldn't persuade my parents. Waiter— champagne, please!"

"Er, not for me, thank you," Jill said to the waiter. "I'd just like a coke."

"Would you like a drink instead?" Paul asked.

"Oh, I don't drink much really," Jill said.

Paul threw his head back and laughed. "You really don't drink? How did you get in with Kyle's group then?"

"Oh, I'm not really in with them," Jill said. "We just got to know each other at a party. I really don't know too many people at Rosemont yet."

"Starting at the top, eh?" Paul said, looking impressed. "If you get in with Kyle you can't go wrong, but you really will have to learn to drink!"

He led her back to Kyle. "Here she is, Kyle—safe and sound."

"Apart from a few broken toes, no doubt," Kyle said dryly. "I bet you're ready for a drink, aren't you?"

"The waiter is bringing me one," Jill said, smiling shyly at the girls who were examining her.

"So who is this, Kyle?" one demanded, slipping her arm through his.

"Oh, this is Jill from school," he said, patting the girl's arm.

"A Rosemont girl, how fascinating," the girl said. "She doesn't look like a brain."

"She's on the newspaper," Kyle said. "She started a riot."

"What fun! Oh, tell us about it." the girls begged.

Kyle did the talking, and Jill was amazed to hear how dramatic he could make a simple food fight sound. The girls looked at Jill with admiration.

Kyle moved away to talk to someone else, and Jill was left with the girls. The talk was all gossip about people she didn't know, and she stood uneasily until Kyle came and rescued her again.

"I don't like dancing much," he whispered, leading her out to the dance floor and then holding her very close. "It seems like such a waste of energy to me. But Paul's mother will lecture me if we don't dance. Besides, I want to work up an appetite before the food is served. Play something to work up an appetite, will you?" he yelled across to the orchestra.

The other dancers laughed, and the orchestra played a faster number. Everyone started dancing, flinging arms and legs in all directions. At the end of the dance everyone was panting, but the only drink being served was champagne. Jill slipped away to find herself a glass of water.

As she opened the kitchen door, four faces looked up suspiciously.

"Can I help you, miss?" the oldest waitress asked.

"Oh, I just wanted a drink of water, thank you," Jill said, walking across to the sink.

"I'll get that for you, miss," the waitress said hastily. "You don't want to splash your pretty dress." She filled a glass for Jill. "Some ice in it, miss?"

"Yes, but I can get it," Jill said, walking toward the refrigerator.

"No, don't bother," the boy waiter said, flinging himself against the refrigerator door. "Let me get it for you."

The other three suppressed giggles.

"He's frightened you're going to find his guilty secret," a waitress suggested.

"Shut up, Christie—whose side are you on?" the boy demanded.

"Oh, don't worry about me," Jill said. "I won't give away secrets. My best friend does waitressing at things like this, and I'm sure she's had loads of guilty secrets by now. I know she dropped a whole salmon mousse one night and had to flush it down the sink!"

The four waitresses started laughing. "You've got a friend who's a waitress?" the older woman asked, surprised.

"She's a student, too," Jill said. "But she needs a part-time job."

"Like Bob," the youngest one said.

"And me," another one added.

"What college is she at?"

"A community college up in Seattle," Jill said.

"Is that where you're from? So what are you doing down here?"

"Christie, don't ask personal questions. Remember, we're the hired help," Bob said, grinning across at Jill.

"My date brought me," Jill explained. "We're at Rosemont together."

"Oh, Rosemont," Christie said, looking impressed. "Isn't that very fancy?"

"I guess so," Jill said. "But there are all sorts of students there. Not everyone is rich."

"Everybody's rich here, for sure. Have you seen the food?" Bob asked.

Christie grinned. "Yeah, we'll do pretty well tonight. We can eat ourselves silly with what they leave here. I won't have to buy food all week!"

"They won't even notice if we help ourselves," Bob agreed. "One of the perks of the job. The employers don't care."

Jill sipped her water. Suddenly she realized that she had been gone a long time and should be getting back.

"Come back to see us again if you get bored out there," Bob said, giving her a wink. "Believe me, these things can get very boring."

As she closed the door behind her, she could hear their laughter. *They seem to be having a better time than the guests*, she thought.

As she came out onto the terrace again, she heard a scream, a splash, and great roars of laughter.

"They threw Melanie in the pool!" a girl was shouting, dancing up and down in delight. "They always throw somebody in the pool!"

172

Jill glimpsed a girl struggling to swim to the side, her full dress floating out like a water lily around her. As Jill watched, a boy yelled, "Don't worry, Melanie, I'll save you," and dived in fully clothed.

"No, you won't, I'll save her," another shouted and dived in from the opposite side. Several others followed, and soon the water was churning as the boys fought over who would bring Melanie to the edge. Jill felt very sorry for poor Melanie and worried that she might get drowned by mistake, since the boys often dragged her underwater as they pulled her toward them.

Finally she shrieked, "Let go of me, I can get out by myself," and dragged herself up the steps.

"I think you're all horrible," she screamed, half sobbing as she wrung water from her dress. "If you think that's funny, then I think you're all crazy. Look at my dress—it's ruined. I only borrowed it, and it's ruined. How can I give it back now? What am I going to tell my friend?" She was crying as two older women led her away.

Jill watched with a lump in her throat. She imagined how she would feel if the same thing had happened to her. The boys were all climbing out, laughing and shouting, not worried at all about their dripping tuxedos.

Paul's mother rushed up and down, saying, "Please go up to Paul's room and get out of those wet things. I don't want anybody coming down with pneumonia at my party!"

As Jill walked away from the pool, she heard one girl say to another, "I always thought she borrowed her dresses."

Suddenly Jill felt lonely and scared as if the girls would look at her next and see that she was wearing her old prom dress. She had been playing a game of make-believe ever since the party at Phillips Hall, trying to make Kyle admire her without considering her own standards. She looked for Kyle and found him sitting with a plate of food at one of the white-clothed tables.

"Oh, there you are," he said. "I wondered where you had gone. Did you see the fun just now? It was magnificent the way she sailed through the air! Here, let me get you some food."

He snapped his fingers and Christie from the kitchen appeared. "This lady would like some food—and make sure you bring her a lot. It's excellent."

"You're not eating," Kyle said later as Jill pushed the food around her plate.

"I'm sorry," Jill whispered. "I'm not really hungry."

He smiled. "Maybe you'll feel like some food later. They've got a cabaret starting in a few minutes."

The cabaret act did begin soon, and the crowd sat through a juggling act that was clever but boring, then a singer, then a magician who produced a live leopard in a cage from nothing. In the middle of the magician's act, Kyle slipped his arm around Jill's shoulder. Jill sat trying to concentrate on the magician. She had let Kyle put his arm around her at the other party, but then she felt safe among familiar faces. This time, the way Kyle stroked her arm made Jill uneasy. Jill was almost ashamed to think of what Craig would say if he suddenly walked into the party.

But the arm around Jill's shoulder seemed to be just a matter of habit for Kyle. After the cabaret, Jill noticed that Kyle held other girls as close as he held her to dance.

Then the dances got slower and slower as the evening progressed. Finally all the couples were dancing with their arms draped over each other's necks. People began to disappear two at a time, and Jill began to worry as she felt Kyle's hand move up and down her back and his warm breath tickle her ear. Perhaps she had encouraged him too much. She had wanted this to be a friendly evening.

"What time were you thinking of driving home?" she asked him casually, pulling back as one dance ended. "People seem to be leaving."

Kyle looked at her with an amused expression.

"I told Paul we'd spend the night here," he said evenly.

"Spend the night here?" Jill blurted out, much louder than she had intended. A couple of people behind them turned around with interest.

"Sure, why not?" Kyle went on. "They have hundreds of bedrooms upstairs. They won't mind and I don't feel like driving all the way back."

"But I didn't bring any night clothes," Jill stammered, embarrassed. Kyle laughed. "You are funny sometimes," he said. "You don't really want to drive home in the dark, do you?"

"I really should get back, Kyle," Jill said, looking down at the ground. "My roommate will think something has happened to me."

"She won't even notice you're missing til morning," Kyle whispered. "And we'll leave nice and early. How about it, Jill? What do you say?"

Jill took a deep breath. "Look, Kyle, I don't want you to get the wrong idea about us," she said. "About our relationship, I mean."

Kyle looked surprised. "What relationship? We only met."

"That's what I mean. I didn't want you to think that I wanted to get involved with you. I already have a boyfriend, Kyle. I can't be more than a friend."

To Jill's amazement and horror Kyle threw back his head and laughed. "I'm not asking you to get engaged, lady," he said. "Which dark ages did you step from?"

Jill was grateful for the darkness so that nobody could see her crimson cheeks. "I'm just not used to this sort of thing, Kyle," she said.

"I can see that," he said sarcastically. "OK, I guess I'd better drive you home, before the princess turns back into Cinderella at midnight!"

Once they were in the car again, Kyle sped wordlessly toward Rosemont. Jill sat silently next to him, afraid that her objections would only cause him to drive faster. He barely slowed down to enter the campus, stopping with a skid in front of Jill's dorm. Before Jill could think of anything to say, he turned and spoke. "Lady, you've got a lot to learn. A lot of guys wouldn't have bothered to bring you home like this. I know you won't thank me, but you ought to."

Jill turned toward Kyle and spoke for the first time since they had left the party. "You're wrong, Kyle. I will thank you—for showing me exactly what kind of person I don't want to be. I do want to have friends and fun and experience new things at college—but not if it means being rude or mistreating other people or pretending to be someone I'm not just to please some spoiled guy who knows nothing about me except that I was a campus celebrity for one day. So, thank you, Kyle, thank you for the most educational experience of my college career."

Before Kyle could respond, Jill pulled open the door of the car and raced up the steps toward her dorm, wiping away large, heavy tears with the back of her hand.

EIGHTEEN

Dear Toni,

I know you'll be pleased to hear that I am cured of ever wanting to belong to the "Beautiful People"! I was so anxious to fit in at Rosemont that I didn't wait to find people like me. I guess I was flattered, too, when Kyle started chasing me. After all, he *is* very good-looking and I could see everyone else would be envious. I never intended to get involved with him, but I can see now that a relationship with someone like him could have been very dangerous for someone like me. He really can be very charming when he wants to. Luckily I saw him at his most uncharming last night when he couldn't get his own way. He wanted us to stay the night at the party. I don't know exactly what that suggestion meant, but I think it meant the worst! I insisted that I wanted to go home.

Before I got out of the car he told me I had a lot to learn. Well, I told him I had learned something, but not in the way he was suggesting. I've discovered that my world is not like his world, and I don't want them to be the same. In fact, I think mine is a lot better, even if it is a little less glamorous.

So now I'm going to take things more gently. After all, I've only been at college six weeks, which isn't long enough to settle into a new place. I like my English class—we're about to read *Pride and Prejudice* by Jane Austen. And I really like the people at the newspaper, although I'll make sure I stick to really harmless articles in the future, such as "Biology Teacher Grows Rare Orchids on Campus." (With my luck they'll discover that the rare orchid is a new type of drug, and I'll be hauled off for questioning by the narcs!)

I hope everything is going well—that your father is back on his feet again and everything is looking up for you. I'm going to start saving so I can come home for a weekend soon. I miss you.

Love, Jill.

Cassandra and Jill were in their room after lunch the next week when there was a frantic tapping on the window, and Robert, who had remained Jill's friend even though her fame had died, appeared, waving an envelope.

"Boy, you really are becoming an old-timer here," he said, laughing as he came inside to hand Jill the letter. "You don't even hang around your mailbox any more! I must be the only one who's still homesick. I have to rush over to that dumb box every day, and I feel totally depressed when there's no mail for me."

Jill smiled. "Don't worry, I feel exactly the same way," she said. "Today must have been the first day I didn't get over there."

Jason appeared behind Robert. "Is it party-time?" he asked. "Is someone offering us coffee?"

"Come on in," Jill said. "I'll make you some."

"Terrific," Jason said, seating himself comfortably on Jill's bed. "The food in the cafeteria is not yet perfect, by a long shot. Did you try the lasagna today? I needed a crane to pick up my plate."

"I have a feeling Jill's activist career is over for a while," Cassandra said. "Today's exposé is on taking advantage of cultural activities on campus— the daily free plays that take place in every classroom when teachers chew up poor freshmen."

"I'll make the coffee," Cassandra said. "You go ahead and read your mail, Jill. I can tell you're dying to."

"Thanks," Jill said. She ripped open the letter and smiled as she read it.

Dear Jill,

Do you realized you are making me write two letters in one year? I'll be in the *Guinness Book of World Records* soon! But I had to write back. To tell you the truth, I was really worried about you going to that party. I've seen the dumb sort of things people do for fun at parties like that, and I didn't want you to get hurt. You don't belong with people who like you because your article made you a star. You need intelligent, together people. In other words, people like me. I'm sure there must be some more of us around the world. Yes, even at Rosemont College. Although please don't like them as much as you like me, OK?

Waitressing is a thing of the past in my life. No, I didn't get thrown out this time. I actually resigned. Can you imagine that? Maybe I'm growing up, too. I talked to an employment agency, and they're sending me out on an interview for a real job. I've got to get out and do something with my life, Jill. I feel I'm about to make a big step forward. I can't tell you any more about it now, but wait for my next important bulletin!

You may be in for a surprise when you come up for a weekend!

More soon. My hand is getting tired.

Luv, luv, luv, Toni.

"News from home?" Robert asked as Jill folded the letter.

Jill nodded. "My best friend. She's just about to get her first real job." Jill wondered what Toni was going to do about college. Had she decided not to go?

"My best friend joined the navy," Robert said. "He's so busy he doesn't even have time to write. We've been best friends since preschool. I don't want to lose touch with him. I mean, Jason here is OK, but I haven't had a chance to train him."

The others laughed as Jason threw a pillow in Robert's direction.

"But what you say is. true," Cassandra said, pouring coffee into four mugs as she spoke. "It's hard to leave friends behind. You wonder if things will ever be the same again when you meet."

"I know," said Jill. "I never thought Craig and I would have trouble finding things to say to each other. But there's so much we have to explain to each other every time we talk on the phone that sometimes it's like talking to a stranger. And it gets even worse when we try to ignore it and pretend everything's normal. I'm not worried, really, but our relationship is definitely going to take more work."

"I just never imagined my best friend and I could end up in such different places," Robert said. "Here I am studying metaphysical poetry while Doug's learning how to run a ship. We may have nothing in common next time we meet."

"I suppose some friendships aren't meant to survive," Cassandra said thoughtfully.

"Oh, but if you're real friends—the sort of friends that Toni and I are—it doesn't matter what different things you do," Jill protested. "I know that when we get together again, it'll be like we've never been away. You just have to be very careful to choose your friends for the right reasons."

"That warms my heart, Jill old friend," Robert said. He sipped his hot coffee. "By the way, good buddy, can I borrow your psych notes from yesterday?"

The four of them laughed as Jill hit him squarely on the head with her remaining pillow.

Look Out!

A SUPER SWEET DREAMS® SURPRISE IS COMING YOUR WAY.

It's the romantic event of the year—the first ever SWEET DREAMS Special Edition. Get to know characters who are just like you and your friends ... Share the fun and excitement, heartache and love that make their lives special.

☐ MY SECRET LOVE: SWEET DREAMS Special Edition #1 is by popular SWEET DREAMS author Janet Quin-Harkin. Laura Mitchell's mother has big plans for her as a belle of Texas high society. But Laura, prefers science fiction books and creative writing to country club events, and she falls in love with a boy from the poorest family in town. So far, she's managed to date Billy Jo secretly, but when he's falsely accused of a crime, Laura knows that only she can prove his innocence. 25884/$2.95

***SWEET DREAMS** Special   You'll never want it to end.*